www.tredition.de

AF204342

Anke Schönle

# A Brighter World

www.tredition.de

© 2019 Anke Schönle

Verlag & Druck: tredition GmbH, Halenreie 40-44, 22359
Hamburg

ISBN
Paperback:   978-3-7497-8388-5
Hardcover:   978-3-7497-8389-2
e-Book:      978-3-7497-8390-8

to all the wonderful people who
encouraged and supported me

# Special Thanks

I've always loved reading the special thanks section in CD booklets (yes, kids, there used to be discs with music on them when I was young), so this is my chance of writing one.

Thank you from the bottom of my heart to:

Fari, without whom I'd never have written this story

Mark, without whom I'd never have published in English

Alex, without whom I wouldn't have *dared* to publish in English—she proofread, commented, asked the right questions, was endlessly kind and patient and *showered* me with praise. Emails from Alex are ego boosts. I consider her a friend and am proud to call her that.

Wendy, who made the cover look pretty. Twice. Well actually *a lot more* than twice… patience of a saint!

Julia, who made *me* look pretty even though I made her take my photo the morning after my fortieth birthday party. She's an angel and a badass.

Taru, my writing comrade. Mutual support means so much!

And last but not at all least my amazing husband Philipp, who put up with a lot of tantrums and me being generally very much in my own world for over a year. I love you.

I love all of you. I am blessed to have you in my life.

# Chapter 1

Alexander Senne opens the file in front of him. It's marked "urgent." He scans the content: twenty-one years old, several cases of shop lifting; fights; in custody because he stabbed a man with a knife. Nothing unusual so far. And then: Stopped eating six days ago; hasn't spoken to anyone since; self harm tendencies.

Alexander picks up his phone and asks the officer to have the detainee brought to him. Once more he reads what little information he has. The picture is inconsistent and fragmentary. He takes a deep breath. New patients *always* make him nervous. That little flutter that he calls stage fright because it feels as if he's about to give a performance. Which is true. First impressions aren't irreversible, but they are important. The kid probably doesn't want to talk to him, and chances are he won't. *The "kid" is twenty-one and dangerous,* Alexander reminds himself. He closes the window and rolls up the sleeves of his shirt. *How symbolic.* He smiles to himself but turns serious the moment there's a knock on the door. Show time.

The kid hasn't said a word, hasn't even looked at him. Slender, bordering on skinny. His long black curls hide his face, and that's not a coincidence. The knuckles of his right hand are bruised. His body language is highly defensive, and he's shaking slightly. His blood sugar must be dangerously low. The kid is starving himself. Alexander hates the idea of force feeding patients, but sometimes there's no other way. The kid isn't very far from that point. Alexander takes a breath. He'll try everything else first.

"What happened a week ago?"

The kid's head snaps up and he stares at Alexander for a moment. He seems confused. *He thinks I should know, that it's on record, whatever it is.*

"Benjamin, I don't know what happened. I won't know unless you tell me."

He's been trying to find out if Benjamin is all right with being called by his first name, but didn't get an answer. So he decided to follow his intuition. They're only nine years apart. It feels like more though. Like Benjamin is younger than his years.


Benjamin Godan looks at Alexander without really seeing him. His jaw tightens, and then he drops his gaze. And suddenly Alexander realises what's happening: Benjamin is fighting tears. Trying to be brave, or tough, not to show any weakness, in the face of someone he doesn't know, doesn't trust. Alexander knows this is it. This is the crucial point. He can wait, or he can push. He leans forward.

"It's your decision, Benjamin," he says very softly. "I want to help you. But you'll have to let me."

"I'm going to jail," Benjamin says between clenched teeth. "People don't usually feel inclined to help me. And why would they."

"You're not convicted yet. And it's my job to help you."

Benjamin doesn't respond, but it's obvious that he's considering. Trying to come to a decision. When he finally does speak, his voice is toneless and so quiet Alexander almost doesn't catch it:

"Eight days ago my mum died. It was an accident, her car—"

His eyes close and his lips form a thin line. He swallows and forces himself to go on:

"She was on her way here. To see me. Dad—they'd had a fight because he didn't want her to visit me. Said I didn't deserve it. She was probably upset and didn't pay attention."

Benjamin looks directly at Alexander, and his pain is almost palpable.

"She died because of me. I lost the only good thing I had left and it's my fault."

Alexander has to take a deep breath not to lose his professional mindset.

"I can help you deal with it. Process your loss."

Benjamin shakes his head.

"I don't need therapy."

Alexander nods at the file on the desk between them.

"You're not behaving exactly sane, are you?"

That was unexpected, Alexander can tell. *Good. Keep him on his toes. Keep him thinking, reacting.* Alexander's voice is calm, but insistent:

"Talk to me. Just a few sessions until you're more stable."

For a long time nothing happens, at least not visibly, but it's obvious to Alexander that something is going on in Benjamin's mind. And then the kid makes a decision. He relaxes just the slightest bit, exhales:

"Fine."

Alexander smiles at him. *There we go.*

## Chapter 2

The next day Benjamin still doesn't say much but eats a bit of breakfast. Their first session is like most first sessions: Alexander explains how things work, tries not to push but makes it clear that he expects Benjamin to cooperate.

"Start small," he says, smiling to himself as he wonders how many times he's said that line before. "You don't have to tell me everything at once. In fact you don't have to tell me everything, period. But do tell me something. Tell me who you are."

"Isn't that in the file?"

"No, it's not. The file is collected data concerning your person. I want to know who you *are*."

"Is there a difference?"

"God yes!"

Benjamin looks puzzled at the fire behind the exclamation. Alexander chuckles.

"Sorry. It's my favourite subject."

When Benjamin just looks at him his smile widens.

"Are you sure you want to get me started?"

The kid looks unsure, but Alexander decides it's as good an opening as any other.

"The central point of my studies was self-awareness. Still is, actually. How a person perceives themselves as opposed to how others do. Or, in addition, to be exact. Have I lost you already?"

"I'm smarter than I look."

Alexander chuckles again.

"I wasn't implying a lack of intelligence. Just a lack of interest. Sorry. Making assumptions is unprofessional."

"So, you want me to tell you something that isn't in my file, but which I personally consider relevant."

*The kid has a way with words.*

"Precisely."

Benjamin takes a breath.

"Well, I would have to know what *is* in the file, wouldn't I?"

Alexander catches himself smiling a lot in this session. Without actually consulting the file he says:

"Son of a retired military officer and an artist, student of English literature, older brother in the Armed Forces."

He pauses for moment before going on.

"Your mother recently passed away. I am very sorry for your loss, Benjamin. Do you want to talk about her?"

"Weren't we supposed to start small?"

Alexander nods.

"OK. So what do I need to know about you?"

Benjamin bites his lip.

"Well, first of all, I'm not really going to uni."

Alexander doesn't react. Just waits.

"I mean I used to, but then — "

He shrugs.

"Did you like it?"

Benjamin looks up, surprised Alexander just lets it rest. Benjamin nods and takes a deep breath.

"Yeah. It's what I've always wanted. Read, write, teach. Literature, theatre. Guess I fucked up pretty spectacularly."

"You can always go back."

"Yeah great. I bet my future students' parents will be thrilled to hand their kids to a criminal."

Alexander is very serious now.

"*If* you are convicted, you will have to work very hard afterwards to earn people's trust. But it's doable."

The kid sits a little straighter.

"Do you really think they will let me do it?"

"Wrong question. Try again."

Benjamin frowns.

"Do I want it bad enough to work for it, not just academically, but personally? Do I think it's worth the effort?"

Alexander makes a gesture that might mean 'there you go' or 'smart kid.'

Benjamin's posture changes again.

"I'm not sure."

"Not sure you want it?"

"Not sure I—well, yeah. I fucked it up. That's it. I'll find something else to do. Possibly legal," he adds as an afterthought.

Alexander calls it a day. He thinks there's something else, something Benjamin isn't telling him, but it's too soon to push him too hard.


Over the next two weeks they talk every other day. Benjamin is eating properly most of the time. A few times Alexander notices fresh bruises on Benjamin's knuckles. But it's getting better. He's more stable, albeit still reserved. Alexander decides it's time to address his education again.

"You said you weren't sure you wanted to go back to uni?"

"I'm not."

Benjamin drops his gaze, playing with the hem of his sleeve.

"Actually—I am. I want to. I just can't."

"What would be necessary for you to be able to do it?"

Benjamin closes his eyes and doesn't say anything for such a long time that Alexander thinks he might refuse to answer the question altogether. And then he realises he's fighting tears.

"Wanna talk about something else?" he says softly.

"What, you just let me off the hook?"

Interesting. He thinks he needs to be pushed. Alexander refuses to comply.

"I'm still easing you in."

That earns him a half smile, but Benjamin is still battling tears.

"I can't do this," he says after a while. His shoulders are tense, defensive.

"Why not?"

"It's pathetic."

"Try me."

The tears are spilling from his still closed eyes now. Alexander gives him time. Doesn't say anything. Benjamin takes a breath and opens his eyes, wiping his face with his sleeve.

"I used to talk to my mother about my studies. She always asked about my exams and papers and what I was reading at the time and she'd remember it all. It—Jesus."

His voice sounds strangled. Alexander knows what's going on. The kid is censoring himself. What he *wants* to say doesn't correspond with the image he's trying to uphold — or maybe even with his self-perception. This is one of the rare occasions a patient *needs* to be pushed.

"It what?"

"It fucking feels like I can't do it without her, OK? Satisfied?"

Benjamin hates him right know, he's aware of that. The kid feels like he's being manipulated into saying something he doesn't want to say. He's openly crying now.

"I miss her, and it feels like a fucking knife wound and yes, I know what that feels like. She's gone because of me and I couldn't even say goodbye and that's my fucking fault as well. I was waiting for my useless shit of a so-called father to lift a fucking finger for me and lo and behold, he didn't. What a surprise."

He takes a few deep breaths, embarrassed about his outburst.

"I guess I'm not making too much sense right now, am I?"

"That's OK. We can sort the pieces later," Alexander says in the light tone that sometimes miraculously comes to him at just the right moments.

Benjamin laughs through his tears, relieved.

"I just barf it all out and we untangle it later? That how it works?"

"Sometimes. Wanna tell me how you feel?"

"Seriously?"

"Seriously."

"Fine—I feel...lighter, I guess. Embarrassed. Upset. But I breathe more freely."

Alexander *likes* this kid. He's a walking contradiction. Smart. Emotional. Eloquent. Witty. And then on the other hand there's aggression, self-harm, arrogance. Alexander hasn't seen that side of him yet, but it's there. The reports add up. He's beaten people up, used a knife at least once. He has a temper that can flare to life in a moment. Why would a young man of Benjamin's abilities fight his way out of tricky situations, use his fists instead of his wits, beat people bloody and sometimes get beaten to a pulp himself, when he could easily talk himself out of them? Again and again?

# Chapter 3

"Why don't we start at the beginning," Alexander suggests.

Benjamin lets out a sigh.

"With the delinquent's troubled childhood? Isn't that a bit of a cliché?"

Alexander chuckles.

"Maybe a little," he admits. "Tell me anyway?"

Benjamin's gaze wanders.

"I'm not sure where to start."

"What's the first thing that comes to your mind when you think of a very young Benjamin?"

"Books. I was always reading, everywhere. Right after waking up, on my way to the bathroom, after breakfast. My mother had to take the book from under my nose or I'd never made it to school."

"Where was your father?"

"Working. He left the house early in the morning and came home late. I didn't get to see much of him."

"How old were you when he retired?"

Benjamin's shoulders tense and he hesitates. It seems odd, given the simple question.

"Fifteen," he says eventually, and something in his voice has changed. Something happened back then, maybe related to his father's retirement, maybe not. Alexander waits. Benjamin takes a deep breath.

"Chris was thrilled about him being at home. That way they could settle the succession together."

His voice is dripping with sarcasm now. Alexander frowns.

"What do you mean?"

"The Colonel was retiring, but he made damn sure the family tradition was passed down."

"Your brother was old enough to join the Armed Forces."

"Exactly. Back then I was convinced he only did it because father had planned it that way. Now I think he really wanted it. He seems to like it."

"Are you close with your brother?"

Benjamin sighs.

"It's — complicated?"

Alexander smiles.

"I barely get to see him. He's Special Forces, Afghanistan right now I believe. He doesn't talk about it."

Benjamin shakes his head.

"It's a completely different world."

"Your father's world?"

"Yeah, exactly. As if those two were speaking a different language from my mother and me. I never got it, and they didn't want me to."

"What did your mother do, did she go to work?"

Benjamin swallows, but then he puts on a brave smile.

"She'd studied voice, but after marrying my father she stopped working. She did sing all the time though."

His smile turns soft.

"When she put us to bed. And while cooking, doing the laundry, driving. Virtually always. When I came home from school I could hear her sing, and I'd know where she was right away."

His eyes are wet. He looks at the floor. Alexander nods.

"Who else plays a role in your life?"

Benjamin blushes a little.

"Well, there's this girl. Angie. We went to school together, and I've always liked her. But we never made it. Also, she's into my brother."

He sits straighter.

"Who's oblivious of course. Idiot."

"Nothing ever happened between the two of you?"

"A bit of flirting, and once we kissed at a party. We were both pretty drunk, and afterwards we pretended it had never happened. Kinda messed up. But she and Chris make a better couple anyway. She briefly considered joining the forces herself."

"You still like her."

Benjamin shrugs.

"Guess that's one more thing I fucked up. She can choose who she wants to be with. I doubt she'll pick an ex-con."

"Who are your friends? Who do you spend your time with?"

Benjamin doesn't say anything for quite a while.

*The look Oli gives him as he is brought to the police station speaks volumes. His best friend has finally given up on him, and that's even worse than the blankness and the shock the first time around. The uniform looks good on Oli. He's well aware of how he must look himself, roughed up and bloody; arrested after a bar fight. The fact that Oli asks a colleague to take his evidence is like a punch to the gut. His oldest friend doesn't even want to be in a room with him.*

Benjamin pulls himself together.

"Fucked that up, too," he murmurs.

"Recently I've mostly been with the *wrong* people I guess," he says and grimaces.

"It began shortly after I'd started uni. My old friends, the ones I'd gone to school with, all did different things, scattered in every direction. At uni there were a few decent people, but I mostly kept to myself."

He runs his hand through his hair.

"Somehow I ended up spending more time in bars than studying, drank a bit too much, one thing led to another —"

*Standing at the bar in his favourite pub. Suddenly there's a hand on his shoulder. He turns and freezes.*

*"Leave me alone."*

*Mark's grin widens. He steps closer. Benjamin starts sweating, his shirt sticking to his back.*

*"I mean it, get lost."*

*"What if I don't?"*

*Faster than he can think his fist connects with that creepy grin. The grin disappears. The next thing Benjamin remembers is someone pulling him away.*

*"You'd better make an exit. Can't be long until the cops show up."*

*Benjamin tries to clear his head. The man lets go of him.*

*"Come on."*

*They leave the pub together.*

*"Mean right hook. I'm impressed," the guy says with a grin. He's older than Benjamin, in his early thirties maybe.*

Benjamin doesn't say much for the rest of the session. There's a lot on his mind, and later he has trouble falling asleep. There's a film playing in his head that he hasn't seen in a while.

# Chapter 4

Alexander is sitting at his desk, typing up his session with Benjamin. He can't get rid of the feeling that something is missing. Something important. A piece of the puzzle, or several pieces, that explain the break in the kid's life. He decides to ask him about the act that brought him into custody. According to the record it was aggravated battery, probably resulting in several years of imprisonment due to his previous convictions. He stabbed a thirty-eight-year-old man with a knife. There are no witnesses to the act itself, but right afterwards two men arrived at the crime scene. They held Benjamin there until the police showed up. The fingerprints on the knife were all Benjamin's. And still there's that nagging feeling that something doesn't add up. Is it just because he likes the kid? Is he simply unwilling to see him as violent?

The next time Benjamin is sitting across the desk from him, he makes a bee line for it.

"Tell me about the crime."

Benjamin rolls his eyes.

"The file is right there."

"You know me. I'd rather hear it from you."

Benjamin folds his arms across his chest.

"A guy messes with me, brawl, guy gets too close, guy takes a knife to his thigh. End of story."

Alexander snorts.

"That was your statement?"

"Basically, yeah, why?"

"Because there's no way in hell I would have believed that."

Benjamin shrugs.

"The pigs did. Sorry. The ladies and gentlemen in law enforcement."

Alexander leans back in his chair. Something is very wrong here. Benjamin plays with his sleeve. He's restless, but he's trying very hard to appear calm. Something is bothering him, and it's very close to the surface.

"I don't believe you. I think the circumstances were different. What I don't get though is why you're lying. Are you protecting the victim?"

Benjamin's facade crumbles. That's it. Alexander takes a deep breath. He leans forward, putting his elbows on the desk.

"Benjamin, you have to testify truthfully! If anything preceded the crime that would clear you, and you're not saying it, you're protecting him! He'll walk, and you'll go to jail. Explain it to me. What happened?"


The kid is white as a sheet.

"I can't."

"Your life depends on it."

Now that gets a reaction. Benjamin looks at him with a raised eyebrow, almost mockingly.

"Isn't that a tad melodramatic?"

"You'd make your life so incredibly hard by spending time in jail. Possibly innocent."

Alexander holds his breath. He's almost certain Benjamin has made a decision. He just needs to act on it now. For an eternity nothing happens. Did the kid make the wrong decision?

And then Benjamin starts to talk:

"I went dancing, on my own. Had a few drinks. The bastard came on to me. I told him he wasn't my type. I thought he'd gotten it, but he hadn't. When I left the club he must have followed me, because all of a sudden I had him around my neck. Literally."

Benjamin's lips are pressed into a thin line.

*Brunner's gasping breath, reeking of beer.*

*"Not your type, my ass. Tight jeans, tight hole. You want this."*

*Brunner's arousal.*

*"You need this, admit it. A real man giving it to you."*

*Panic. Benjamin can't breathe. And then, all of a sudden, the slightest bit of space. Not enough to wrestle himself free. But enough to get to his knife and blindly stab his attacker.*

Benjamin's breathing is shallow and his voice strained:

"He would have just fucked me through the floor if I hadn't gotten hold of my knife. He described it to me in detail. I was supposed to suffer as much as possible. Satisfied?"

His face is a mask of disgust. He's shaking. Alexander closes his eyes. He needs a few moments to distance himself from Benjamin's emotions.

"That's self defence, Benjamin," he says eventually. "You were defending yourself against an attempted rape. That's not indictable."


Benjamin amends his testimony. Two more men incriminate Brunner. Benjamin is discharged.

"Thank you. For everything," he tells Alexander as they say goodbye.

Alexander nods and smiles at him.

"Take this," he says and holds out a business card.

"Call me at my practice if you feel you need a little more support."

Benjamin takes the card.

*There's a 50/50 chance he'll do it,* Alexander thinks. *It would do him good.*

## Chapter 5

Benjamin decides to continue therapy. When they shake hands, Alexander notices fresh bruises on Benjamin's knuckles. Both hands, not just his dominant right.

"What happened?"

"My father drives me insane."

Alexander frowns.

"Don't worry, we didn't fight."

"You've started harming yourself again. Like you did in detention, fists against a wall," Alexander assumes.

Benjamin pulls his sleeves down over his hands.

"Let me see."

Benjamin hides even more deeply in his jumper.

"Please?"

Alexander looks at him. Reluctantly Benjamin pushes the sleeves back. Alexander takes his left hand and turns his palm up. The sleeve slides back even further.

"These are old," he states calmly. "Burns and cuts, scratches maybe."

Benjamin pulls his hand away. The sleeve slides in place and covers his scars. Alexander looks at him.

"How old?"

Benjamin averts his gaze.

"Six years."

Alexander doesn't say anything, he just waits. And then Benjamin starts talking, his eyes on the floor.

"Back then everything was suddenly different, like the rug was pulled out from under my feet. And when I burned or scratched or cut myself, didn't really matter which, I felt—I don't know, grounded?"

"You were in control. That was the one thing in your life you could control. How bad the pain would be. How long it would last."

Benjamin looks up. He seems surprised. Alexander smiles at him.

"Accurate?"

Benjamin nods.

"I guess. When you put it like that it makes sense."

"Do you want to tell me why you're doing it again—or why you did it back then?"

Benjamin gives him a half smile.

"Neither?"

Alexander chuckles.

"You know the rules."

Benjamin is struggling. Alexander waits. Eventually Benjamin takes a deep breath.

"When I was fifteen I found out that my parents weren't really my parents. I'm adopted. For fifteen years my so-called parents didn't see fit to inform me of that detail."

His voice sounds bitter. The pain of that discovery is still fresh even six years later.

"My mother wanted another child. My father… I think he agreed to the adoption like other people buy their wife a dog. And just like a dog he would have gotten rid of me later if he could have. I must have been a horrible disappointment for him. We have nothing in common. After I'd found out, I wondered why I hadn't noticed it myself. It was pretty obvious actually."

"Are you anything like your mother?"

Benjamin closes his eyes. After a while he nods.

"But I couldn't have one without the other."


*"He's not my father!"*

*"Am I not your mother then?"*


"If I hadn't respected him as my father, I'd have lost her, too."

The words are hanging in the air like a verdict. Alexander takes a breath to get rid of the tightness in his chest.

"Do you have good memories of your father? Just one?"

It takes a while, but then Benjamin smiles. His features turn soft, and he looks incredibly young.

"We went for a walk in the woods, in winter, the whole family. Usually my father wouldn't have joined us, but that day he did. He held Chris' hand and mine, too, a son on each side. That once I mattered just as much as my brother."

His smile widens.

"He showed us some tracks in the snow. They were a hare's. I knew that because we'd talked about it in school. It made him happy, and I was so proud. The next day I borrowed a book about animals from the library and learned all the animals' tracks by heart."

His smile dies.

"Of course we never again went to the woods together."

They're both silent for a long time. Eventually Alexander asks:

"Do you know anything about your birth parents?"

Benjamin shakes his head.

"Didn't care. They didn't want me. That's all I need to know."

Alexander shrugs.

"Maybe you'd understand their reasons?"

"What's to understand? My mother dropped me and wanted to get rid of me as quickly as possible. End of story."

Alexander doesn't comment, but he's not convinced that's the whole truth.

# Chapter 6

One day Benjamin is a bit early for his appointment and overhears a heated discussion – taking place behind closed doors but loud enough for him to recognise it as a couple having a fight. Alexander Senne sounds pretty angry... the last thing Benjamin hears is:

"...and don't you dare show up here again!"

The door bursts open – and a man the same age as Senne storms past Benjamin. Benjamin looks after him for a moment before slowly turning around to face Alexander who's standing in the door to his office. He looks exhausted.

"I'm sorry, Benjamin. I told him a thousand times not to come here."

Benjamin needs a moment.

"Boyfriend?" he finally manages.

"Ex," Alexander says, and there's a lot of baggage in that one syllable.

Benjamin swallows.

"If this is a bad time..."

Alexander pulls himself together.

"That's all right. We do have an appointment."

"Are you sure?"

Alexander smiles.

"Yes. I am. Come in."

Benjamin is less cooperative than usual. Not necessarily closed off or defensive, but weirdly distant. Alexander decides he has to address it.

"Are you upset about the fact that I'm gay?"

Benjamin clearly doesn't know what to say.

"Be honest with me, please."

"I don't know. I guess, yeah. I'm not sure why though."

"What's your idea of a gay man?"

"Huh?"

"We all have certain stereotypes, even if we're not aware of them. Opinions we've heard from others. Public perception. If yours don't line up with your perception of me, it might confuse you. It can be unsettling."

"That—makes sense, but that's not it. I think. I mean, if I gave a single fuck about what my father thinks—which luckily I don't—"

He sighs.

"I think it's about something else. There's something I never told you, because I'm so used to hiding it. I've defended it with my fists more than once. And now you just tell me I can – I mean you've always told me I can talk about anything, but –"

He runs a hand through his hair.

"I guess I should just say it, right? Bisexual. That's my label, and I hate it. I tried really hard not to be that. To focus on girls. But it doesn't work that way."

He closes his eyes and tips his head back.

"Shakespeare was bi." he says in a strange, almost amused voice.

Alexander smiles.

"I know. Some of his most beautiful sonnets are about this young man he was in love with who was stolen from him by another man with more money."

Benjamin smiles, his eyes still closed. After a long silence he says:

"I feel like there's a whole world inside my mind that nobody knows about, that I've never talked about, to anybody, and you just broke down that door."

"Does that scare you?"

"Shitless."

"Couldn't it be a chance, too?"

Benjamin opens his eyes but stares at the ceiling.

"I'm not sure I need more complications in my life."

"You don't have to come out if you don't want to."

Benjamin looks at him.

"I thought you'd tell me to. Be honest, admit it."

"To yourself? Absolutely. Publicly? That's a huge step and not always the best course of action."

The kid is processing.

"Wouldn't that be kinda gutless?"

"It might be necessary if you're in an unsafe situation."

Benjamin doesn't say anything for a long time. Alexander realises that he's found the missing piece. Benjamin had to learn the hard way not to show weakness. The fights. The aggression towards anyone who would question his tough image. Self defence all along. Alexander takes a breath.

"Did anyone ever treat you inappropriately before? Teacher? Family member? Anyone?"

"What, I'm an abuse victim now? Like do I attract those creeps on a regular basis?"

"That's not a thing. And you don't have to answer anything you don't want to, you know that."

The kid is clearly upset, but there's no way of telling if it's because of what Brunner did to him or something else, something more, something older. Alexander has a hard time keeping his own emotions in check. Benjamin is more vulnerable right now than he's ever seen him. He needs stability, reliability, professional detachment. Calmness. Alexander relaxes.

"Is there anything else you need to get off your chest right now?"

"What, not enough drama for one session?"

Not his usual charming wit, but a trace of menace. Provocation. Alexander doesn't bite.

"You tell me."

Benjamin deflates. He looks very tired all of a sudden. Exhausted.

"I guess I have a lot of thinking to do."

Alexander smiles at him and reaches into his top drawer. He takes out a business card and writes something on the back.

"I rarely do this, but in case you need to talk to me outside of business hours..."

Benjamin turns the card in his hands. Private mobile phone number. Alexander can count the number of patients he's given it to on one hand.

"Thanks," Benjamin says, and his voice sounds strangled. "I appreciate it. Promise I won't use it unless absolutely necessary."

Alexander catches a glimpse of the kid's eyes. They're suspiciously bright. He realises he might be the only person Benjamin can talk to, and his loneliness breaks his heart.

"Tell you what. Why don't we meet *before* next Tuesday? I think you might need the extra session. What do you think?"

Benjamin nods.

"Thanks. Yeah, I think that's a good idea."


After the session Benjamin barely makes it to his car before the movie in his head starts playing.

*A party at the dorm.*

*"Benjamin, isn't it?"*

*Sparkling blue eyes and three–day–old stubble.*

*"Erm, yeah? Do I know you?"*

*"We have a few courses together, but I don't think you've ever noticed me. You're always so focused."*

*They have a drink together, and they talk.*

*"I've never seen you with anyone… girlfriend?"*

*Ben smiles.*

*"No."*

*"Boyfriend?"*

*Ben's gut clenches. His face is burning. He swallows and shakes his head.*

*"Oh, sorry – I'm Mark."*

*They have a few more drinks but don't talk much. Instead they keep glancing at each other and smile a lot. Mark looks at him for a long moment.*

*"Can I kiss you?" he says softly.*
*Ben's stomach does a somersault. He nods before he has a chance to overthink. Mark's kiss is gentle, careful. He's waiting for Ben's reaction. And Ben does react. It feels like coming home. He's losing himself in the kiss, enjoying Mark's tenderness. He didn't think it could feel like this. With a man. They look at each other. Mark is beaming. Ben grins—and kisses him again.*

*Mark's room. Ben's head is spinning. He can't remember feeling like this ever before. Mark's hands wander over Ben's shoulders as they are kissing. He pulls Ben's t-shirt over his head and opens Ben's belt. Ben panics.*

*"Wait," he pants.*

*Mark frowns.*

*"Come on, don't tell me you don't want this."*

*His puts his hand on Ben's jeans and grins.*

*"Pretty obvious, don't you think?"*

*Ben retreats.*

*"Don't."*

*"There are other ways," Mark murmurs right into Ben's ear. All of a sudden Ben is on his knees. He can't remember how that happened. He can't breathe, tries to get up. Mark grabs his shoulders.*

*"It's the least you can do!"*


*Ben barely realises what he's doing, but his lips find the way. Mark's head falls back with a moan.*

*"So good," he whispers. "Come on, don't stop."*


*There's no warning. Ben manages to swallow just in time. He's crouched on the floor, trying to process what just happened. Mark bends down and kisses him. This kiss feels different than the others, as if Mark doesn't need Ben's permission any longer. As if he can just take what he wants now.*

*Ben runs from the dorm and ends up at a bar. His first time with a man, and he feels horrible, used and filthy. He should have said 'No' sooner. Or more firmly. Is it his fault that things went the way they did? He drinks a lot more than usual. The bar is crowded. He pushes against someone, one word leads to another, and all of a sudden, fists are flying. Ben finds himself on the street. His face and ribs hurt, and so does his hand. He throws up, crouched in a corner, panting — and feels more miserable than ever before in his life.*

*When he wakes up in his bed at the dorm, he can't remember how he made it home. It's almost noon. He's supposed to be at uni. There was something important today.*

*Mark blocks his way on the stairs.*

*"You coming to my room?"*

*His grin is complacent and unsettling.*

*"No, thanks." Ben says and tries to get past him. Suddenly Mark is very close, pushes him against the wall.*

*"Come on," he whispers, "you want it. You need that, someone to put you in your place. You looked good on your knees."*

*Mark grabs his crotch. Ben manages to free himself, but Mark's laughter follows him, scornful and threatening. Ben tries to shed the memory of Mark's touch, but he can't.*

It takes Benjamin a long time until he's able to drive.

# Chapter 7

Three days later Benjamin tells Alexander about all of his crushes, male and female. It turns out most of them were women, and now he's unsure if he's even really bi.

"There's no quota for being bi, Benjamin. If it's how you identify, it's valid."

"What about you?"

Benjamin bites his lip, realising he probably crossed a line. Alexander makes a conscious decision to be more open than usual.

"What *about* me?"

"Have you ever been attracted to a woman?"

"Not really. I thought I was a few times but that was probably just me trying to be like everybody else. It's always been men for me."

"When did you come out?"

"To my parents—very early. They have always been supportive. And from then on out it was more or less a known fact."

"It sounds so easy when you talk about it."

"I was very privileged. It's different for everybody. And remember you don't have to come out. You don't owe anything to anyone. If there's one person you trust, tell them. And only them."

"I would like to tell Angie." Benjamin says very softly.

"I'm not even into her any more, but she's a good person. I think she'd understand. With my brother I'm not so sure. And my father would kill me with his bare hands and make the body disappear."

It's supposed to sound light-hearted, but the lifelong hurt is obvious. He's never been right, never been good enough in his father's eyes. It's the trauma of Benjamin's life, balanced a little by his mother's love as long as she was alive. Now there is nothing.

"So talk to Angie. What do you think she will do?"

"Hug me, probably. She's such a hugger. It's her solution for everything."

"And how do you feel about that?"

"I think it might be nice. Human touch. You know."

He blushes most adorably.

"Not, like, sexual. Just —"

He shrugs. Alexander feels his chest tighten. The kid is so hungry for affection.


During their next session Benjamin tells Alexander that Angie is about to leave town for a new job. He says he considered telling her anyway but 'chickened out'. Alexander takes a good look at the kid. He dresses completely in black these days and tends to be wrapped up in at least four layers, one of them usually leather. He's still fragile, still skinny, but more or less stable. Hasn't been in trouble with the police ever since he was released, and his self destructive behaviour has gone down significantly. Generally the last sessions were very productive, and even considering the Angie set back, he's headed in the right direction. And still that makes what has to come next no easier. Alexander clears his throat.

"Listen, Benjamin, there's something I have to tell you. I'm afraid I won't be able to continue with our sessions, but I've spoken to a colleague of mine. She agreed to take over from me, if you want to, of course. But I think you'll like her."

Benjamin freezes. Alexander isn't sure he's breathing.

"What? I mean — why? Did I do something wrong?"

Alexander stares at him for a moment and then shakes his head.

"No!"

He runs a shaking hand through his hair and collects himself.

"Actually, I need to tell you something, and no matter your reaction, it'd be unethical if — "

He sits straighter and puts his hands in his lap. Damn shaking.

"I can't keep working with you because I'm attracted to you. I like you a lot and maybe — "

He takes a deep breath. This is nothing like what he prepared.

"I'm sorry if this is too sudden. But I wanted to be honest with you."

Benjamin is stunned speechless. And then his shoulders tense and he stands. For a moment Alexander thinks he'll simply leave. But he doesn't.

"So that's it. *You* decide this is over. After all the talk you've given me about working on my trust issues. You've told me I could rely on you, over and over again until I finally, stupidly, did. And now you throw me out because you can't be bothered to keep your libido in check."

The disgust in the young man's eyes is more painful than any reaction Alexander imagined. He closes his eyes for a moment, trying to find something to say. But Benjamin is right. He's abandoning him. One more person failing him.

"I'm sorry," that's all he can get out. *I don't know what to do*, he wants to say, but doesn't, *I'm falling for you*. That's his problem though, not Benjamin's.

"Please talk to Mrs Miller", he says instead, holding out a business card.

"Did you make sure I'm not her type?" Benjamin spits out.

There's nothing Alexander can say to that, and he's barely keeping it together until Benjamin has left. And then Benjamin's gone and Alexander realises he might never see him again, and he starts wondering if he's done the right thing.


Benjamin leans against the wall of the building, the city's noises washing over him. *I'm not allowed to talk to Alexander Senne any more.* That's the only thing on his mind, over and over again. Losing this haven hurts so much he can barely keep the tears in check. He winces at the things he's just thrown at Senne, aware that what he said, the way he said it, was unfair. But he was simply lashing out like he's always done when he got hurt. And no way is he going to start all over again with a new therapist, open up again, just do be let down again. If he loses what they have achieved it's on Senne. *Yeah, right, as if he'll ever know. Or care.*

*Benjamin is staring at Alexander, trying to process what he's just told him. When he finally finds his tongue the first thing he says is:*

*"You know everything about me."*

*"I know that's tricky, and I'm sorry if it feels weird."*

*"No, I mean, with everything I've told you – why would you like me?!"*

*Alexander smiles at him, warm and open, and thinks that he's never looked at Benjamin like that before.*

*"You're amazing, Benjamin Godan. You're razor blade sharp and incredibly observant, and you're sensitive and passionate and drop dead beautiful."*

*That makes Benjamin blush. He looks down for a moment and then up at Alexander through his lashes, and Alexander has to take several steadying breaths at the sight.*

*"Don't say anything right now. Think about it. Let me know when you're ready. OK?"*

*Benjamin smiles, and Alexander can't help but feel a little hurt at the relief on the young man's face.*

*"OK," Benjamin says and gets out of his chair. "I will."*

Some of Alexander's dreams are more vivid. Fantasies, not all of them in his sleep. The few times he allows himself to indulge in them he feels horribly guilty afterwards.

# Chapter 8

*Seven years later*

*Alexander*'s best friend Paul is grinning into his beer. Alexander looks at him quizzically.

"What?"

"I think there's a bit of drool on your shirt."

"Huh?"

"Whoever it is you've been staring at, he must be quite the sight."

Alexander blushes.

"Don't turn. At the bar."

Of course Paul turns.

"I said — " Alexander sighs in frustration.

"What, black hair, leather jacket?"

"M-hm."

"Go talk to him. I can vanish if you want."

"No!"

Paul stops grinning.

"Oh no. You know him!"

"I do. It was a century ago though."

"So, you two...?"

"No. Nothing ever happened. I just had a major crush on him."

"And he wasn't interested?"

"It's complicated."

"Isn't it always?"


There's no doubt. Alexander recognises Benjamin's eyes right away as well as his killer cheekbones. His features are still delicate, but not quite as fragile as they used to be. And he's bulked up a little. Still slender, but with broader shoulders. It suits him just as well as the shorter hair, his curls tamed by a bit of hair gel, but not long enough for a ponytail any more. He's gorgeous. And he's looking straight at Alexander. *Crap.* Benjamin slides off his stool and comes over, and Alexander's palms are getting sweaty. He stealthily wipes them on his jeans.


"Mr. Senne!"

"Please call me Alexander," he manages, and out of the corner of his eye he notices Paul making an exit.

Benjamin smiles and gives him a graceful little nod.

"Alexander."

Then he remembers the way they parted. There's an awkward silence. Alexander recovers first. Smiling at Benjamin he says:

"You look great! What have you been up to?"

"Went back to uni. I just passed my exams. Today I got my stuff from my dad's house."

He gestures at the bottle in his hand.

"Needed a beer after an evening with him."

Alexander winces.

"Still that bad?"

Benjamin heaves a sigh.

"He won't change. That's OK, I'll be gone tomorrow and don't have to come back ever again."

Alexander nods at Benjamin's almost empty beer.

"Can I buy you another one?"

"I'm driving." Benjamin shrugs apologetically.

It hurts. Alexander has just met him again, and now he's about to lose him for good.

"I see," he hears himself say, when actually what he really wants to say is '*Please don't walk out of my life again*'.

He smiles at him.

"You've come such a long way."

"And in no small part thanks to you."

Alexander turns his own beer in his hands. He can't make eye contact right now.

"You were so angry at me back then, and rightly so."

Benjamin sighs.

"I was, actually, for a while. You were the one person in my life I could rely on, and suddenly—"

"I abandoned you. One more person in your life who failed you."

Alexander's voice is barely audible over the noise of the busy bar.

"Still, I'm sorry. I had no right to say the things I said. What else were you supposed to do?"

"I really don't know. I didn't know what to do. I knew I was hurting you, and that was the last thing I wanted, but I just—"

"It's OK, Alexander, really. I'm good."

Alexander doesn't tell him how long it took him not to check for a text first thing in the morning. How long it took for the disappointment to stop every time his phone pinged and it was someone else. Alexander pushes himself to make one last attempt:

"Need any help moving?"

Benjamin hesitates for a fraction of a second. It's enough for Alexander's heart to sink. But then Benjamin smiles at him, an open, radiant smile Alexander has rarely ever seen on him. *Good Lord the guy is beautiful.*

"One can never have enough help when moving, right?"

## Chapter 9

Which is why the next day Alexander finds himself in the middle of a whirl-wind operation. Chris, Angie and what feels like half a dozen of Benjamin's fellow students are talking, laughing and joking—and almost in passing they get Benjamin settled in. By the time Alexander finds a minute to pause and look around, all the furniture is assembled and in place and Benjamin has even started to unpack a few boxes. There are hugs and thank-yous and see-you-soons—and all of a sudden it's just Alexander and Benjamin.

"I need a drink," Benjamin proclaims. "Did you happen to see my wine glasses?"

Alexander didn't, and neither of them can be bothered to look for them, so they end up drinking the wine one of Benjamin's friends brought from mismatching mugs. Alexander's reads, 'My brother went to Afghanistan and all I got...' Benjamin's simply says, 'Shakespeare nerd.'

"So, what's next?" Alexander asks after a while.

"What, haven't I exploited you enough?"

Alexander chuckles.

"I meant, for you."

"School starts in two weeks, so I'll unpack all the books and get started with my preparations. Also there's a project I've been working on that I hope to get done in time."

"Can you tell me?"

"Hey, Chris is the one with the classified missions. I'm just an English teacher."

Benjamin pauses and starts to smile.

"Is it silly how much I like the sound of that?"

Alexander's stomach does a somersault.

"Not at all," he says very gently. "I bet you'll be amazing. Your students are going to love you."

"Until I start torturing them with blank verse."

They both grin at that.

"So — what's that project?"

"You're not easily distracted, are you?"

"Nope."

Benjamin seems shy all of a sudden, which makes him look a lot younger than he is. And reminds Alexander of a time he wasn't supposed to look at the guy but still did. Benjamin senses the change in Alexander's mood right away.

"What's wrong?"

Alexander shakes it off.

"I'm good. Stop stalling."

"OK… so, I kinda rewrote Henry IV."

"You what?"

"I thought, 'Why are students so reluctant to read Shakespeare?' and obviously it's because he's hard to understand if you're not used to his language — but the stories themselves are great! So—I rewrote it. A rebellious young prince with shady friends and severe daddy issues in modern English. What's not to love?"

Alexander thinks nervous Benjamin is the most adorable thing ever and barely refrains from telling him so. *Oops. Easy on the wine.*

"Read it to me?"

"It's not finished."

"Please?"

Benjamin swallows.

"I'll need *a lot* more wine for that."

"As thou wisheth, Your Grace," Alexander declares and refills Benjamin's mug.

"You know, that's actually not—anyway. I'll go find it. Might take a moment though."

He disappears to his bed-room and takes his wine with him. Alexander drains his mug and looks around. Benjamin's CD shelf is already assembled and half full. He looks at the titles and takes one or two albums from the shelf. When Benjamin finally shows up again, script in hand, Alexander turns around and holds up a CD.

"One of these things is not like the others." He grins and raises his eyebrows. "Brahms?"

Benjamin takes the CD from him and puts it back.

"That's my mother's choir. I can't listen to that, but I can't get rid of it either."

Alexander bites his lip.

"I'm sorry." he says softly.

"It's OK. You couldn't know."

Benjamin takes a deep breath and holds up his script.

"Are you sure you wanna hear this?"

"Absolutely sure," Alexander says and refills his mug.


Alexander listens to Benjamin's rich baritone like one listens to music. After the first awkward moments Benjamin warms for his subject and makes little remarks as he goes. It's easy to imagine him in front of a class. If only his own English teacher had been anything like Benjamin… it belatedly registers with him that Benjamin has stopped reading and is grinning from ear to ear.

"What?"

"You'd probably planned that as an internal monologue," he says dryly, still grinning like the cat that got the cream. Alexander blushes scarlet.

"I did not just—"

"Yup. What were they like?"

"Huh?"

"Your English teacher!"

Alexander buries his face in his hands.

"It's the wine," he slurs.

When there's no answer, he lifts his head. Benjamin's whole posture has gone soft and gentle. So is his voice:

"I was kinda hoping it wasn't."

Alexander freezes, unable to speak, unable to think. Benjamin bites his lip.

"I mean, back then—you liked me. It's been a long time, but—"

And then his courage fails him. Alexander can see him retreat, girding himself against rejection. If he was wearing his beloved leather jacket he'd put the collar up and zip it up. As it is there's only an old black hoodie to hide in, and he does, hands buried in the pockets and his chin tucked in. *Talk, Alex, for crying out loud, before Benjamin just dissolves out of embarrassment.* But he can't. His brain isn't processing the fact that Benjamin might be interested. He's spent too much time trying not to think about the guy. Benjamin straightens a bit.

"I'm sorry. It probably *is* the wine. I shouldn't have assumed—"

He takes a breath.

*God, the bravery!* Alexander thinks, but he still can't say anything.

"Anyway, thank you for helping us today."

*No. No no no no no! Work, stupid brain! Say something. Anything.* But nothing comes to mind. He instinctively reacts to Benjamin's dismissive body language and stands with him. And then he looks at Benjamin and starts shaking.

"Alexander? Are you OK?"

"No!"

*Finally!*

"I'm so not OK, I don't even have words for it!"

Benjamin puts his hands on Alexander's shoulders.

"You're scaring me."

And that does it. Like a slap to his face or a bucket of ice water those words finally kick his brain into gear.

"I'm in awe of you, Benjamin! You're amazing, and I'm falling for you all over again. I'm an idiot for letting you think, even for a moment, that I'm over you. I'm sorry. God I'm so sorry!"

Benjamin starts to laugh. A low chuckle that turns into a full belly laugh, complete with tears and sobs, and Alexander joins in because it's infectious. When they finally calm down, Benjamin takes that one step closer and pulls Alexander into a hug.

"You *are* an idiot, Mr. Therapist."

"I am. I'm sorry."

"Yeah, we established that."

Benjamin lets go and looks at him.

"Can I kiss you, please?"

Alexander just nods, and then there's nothing but this amazing young man, soft and strong at the same time, insecure and cheeky and brilliant and oh so beautiful, and Alexander loses himself in the kiss.

# Chapter 10

They are sitting on the couch, surrounded by boxes, their now empty mugs set aside on top of one that reads 'kitchen.' Benjamin's head has fallen back and his eyes are closed, which gives Alexander a chance to study him. He looks relaxed. Exhausted, but content.

"Are you excited to start teaching?"

Benjamin just smiles without changing his posture.

"I am. I've done it before, you know, while I was still studying. But now it's for real. My responsibility. I like it — and it scares me a little."

"All the best things start that way," Alexander says, and it's only after he said it that he realises he might be talking about something more than just teaching. Benjamin senses it, too. He looks at Alexander with a small smile that Alexander remembers well.

"I know nothing about you," he states, and it sounds a little surprised.

"What do you want to know?"

And there it is. The smile turns smug.

"Let me think — tell me something about yourself that you consider relevant."

Alexander bursts out laughing.

"You've been paying attention."

"I am very observant. Or so I'm told."

Alexander gives him a warm smile.

"You are. It's a beautiful quality, especially for someone working with young people."

"Right now I am observing that you are avoiding the question."

Alexander grins.

"Sorry. Got caught up in your glow. What was the question?"

"Seriously?"

Alexander shrugs. Benjamin shakes his head with a wide smile.

"Tell me about yourself. What do I need to know?"

"Oh, right. My favourite subject."

Benjamin rolls his eyes. Alexander takes a breath.

"OK... I come from a family of doctors. My Granddad was a genius. The way he talked about the human body and its mechanics fascinated me. I spent hours with his anatomy books long before I could read. I knew a ton of medical terms by the time I started school. I would lay on the floor in his study with his books, and every time I came across something I didn't understand, or something that grossed me out, he'd explain it. Draw me pictures. Find me illustrations. I learned cross referencing at an early age — and also that there's rarely ever only one truth."

"Sounds like a happy childhood."

There's no bitterness in Benjamin's voice. Alexander looks him squarely in the eye.

"I was a very happy child, growing up in a loving, supportive family. I was very, very lucky."

Benjamin looks like he's about to say something but doesn't for a long moment.

"So, what made you choose psychology over medicine?"

"Fate, if you wanna call it that." Alexander sighs. "I started studying medicine. My dad is a surgeon, I wanted to follow in his footsteps. He once told me about that special state of mind he's in when he operates—like a tunnel. All focused on the task at hand. It sounded so powerful, and at the same time he was completely humble about it. I wanted that. Knowledge. Skill. Power, too. But in a good way, using it to help and heal… anyway. After the first semester I had a skiing accident."

Alexander studies his hands.

"Complicated fractures in both hands. Tendon rupture in my right hand. I spent an eternity in therapy, but it became clear that I wouldn't be able to handle a scalpel. They still start shaking when I'm stressed. I can control it to a certain degree, but—"

He takes a breath.

"Pretty much the low point of my life. Good thing we got that out of the way on the first date," he says with a shrug that poorly disguises his true feelings.

Benjamin winces.

"I'm sorry. I didn't mean—"

"It's fine. It was my decision to tell you. And I was serious. I think it's a good thing that you get to see me like that."

"Because you've seen *me* that way. More than once."

"Yeah."

Alexander takes another breath.

"Anyway. My mother's best friend is a psychologist, so Mum had that idea. At first it felt like a consolation prize. Which, funnily enough, is exactly what my best friend Paul kept teasing me about: him becoming a *real* doctor while I was just faking it. But soon I was as fascinated with Psychology as I had been with medicine, maybe even more. Throughout all my years at uni my dad and granddad would ask me about my studies. They wanted my take on 'today's case' as we called it. It made me realise the significance of psychology as a part of the human condition, in addition to the physical, *underneath* the physical."

He smiles a little sheepishly.

"Sorry. Got carried away."

When he meets Benjamin's eyes there's nothing but warmth.

"You have nothing to be sorry about. I could listen to you talk about your job all day. Such passion. That's very attractive."

Alexander ducks his head.

"Isn't it—weird? For you? I mean, given how we met and all?"

Benjamin nods.

"Yeah. It is, if I think about it too much. On the other hand, I owe you so much for that time. I was a mess. You fixed me."

"Oh no. That is *not* how it works."

"You know what I mean. I couldn't have done it on my own."

Alexander looks at him for a moment.

"You're welcome," he says softly.

For a while neither one of them says anything, both of them lost in thought, and then Benjamin smiles.

"I did have a crush on you, you know?"

Alexander's head snaps up.

"You what?"

"I wasn't sure what it was. Gratitude, dependence, infatuation, I don't know. I hadn't been attracted to a guy in forever. I wasn't even sure I was into men any more. But I felt something for *you*. Because you were there for me, always calm, never mean. You were the one I talked to about everything. But that meant that I had no one to talk to about *you*. Most people I knew would have beaten the shit out of me for even looking at a man, and those who might have tolerated it would have frowned upon the therapist/patient thing. I was completely alone with that problem."

"And then I threw you out."

"And then you threw me out, yeah."

Alexander moves closer to Benjamin on the couch, turning his body towards him.

"I don't have words to apologize for that, Benjamin."

"You've explained it, more than once, and I understand. There wasn't a good solution to that dilemma. Other than not falling in love. But who can blame you."

They both realise how that sounded at the same time and burst out laughing. Benjamin is wiping away tears as he tries to get his breathing under control.

"I meant—"

"Who can blame me for falling in love with *this*!" Alexander exclaims, gesturing at Benjamin with both hands.

"I *meant*," Benjamin tries again, "that you can't control who you fall for."

"I got you," Alexander says softly. "Believe me, I tried. All the different stages were there. Ignorance, denial, resistance. The night I finally admitted to myself that I was falling in love with you I got so drunk I had to call in sick the next morning. I didn't know what to do. Or, actually, I did. There was only one thing I could do and still be able to look at myself in the mirror."

After a short pause Benjamin says:

"It's OK, Alexander. Stop beating yourself up over it. There was no other way. And I lived."

"You never contacted my colleague."

"Did you keep tabs on me?"

"I asked her once or twice. She said she never heard from you."

"I didn't think I needed it, to be honest. I was doing OK. Getting back into uni was the best thing I could do. New people. A change of scenery. And I was doing what I love, what I'm good at. I did take a few sessions of counselling on campus. I was fine. I am fine, Alexander. Can you please stop worrying about me?"

"Never."

The smile that one word evokes just screams for a kiss. Being fussed over is so unfamiliar to Benjamin that it throws him off balance, but Alexander can tell that he likes it. He frames Benjamin's face with both hands, and yes, they are shaking a little.

"I will never stop worrying about you," Alexander whispers against Benjamin's mouth, "because you deserve it."

This kiss is different from their first one. There's a promise in it, assurance. It feels like the first step of a journey.

# Chapter 11

Over the next two weeks Alexander doesn't get to see as much of Benjamin as he would like to, because the soon-to-be teacher is buried over his head in his books. They text each other a few times a day. The night before school starts Benjamin's nervousness is palpable over the screen of Alexander's phone.

A: Do you want me to come?

B: Nah, not necessary. I'll call it an early night.

A: It's 11:48 already.

B: I'm in bed already.

A What are you wearing?

A: Just kidding.

Benjamin sends a grinning emoji.

B: Wouldn't you like to know.

Five minutes pass. They both stare at their phones. Alexander hits 'call.'

"Hey."

"Hey. I can't stop thinking about you in bed. I don't know what to say that wouldn't sound weird. More weird."

He sighs.

"But I hate that you're there and I'm here. I'd rather be with you."

Benjamin is awfully quiet.

"Benjamin? Are we good?"

"I'm trying to make up my mind."

"About what?"

"About what I want."

Alexander turns pale.

"What do you mean?"

There's another pause.

"I'd rather you were here with me, too, I think."

Alexander starts breathing again.

"So I'll come."

"It's almost midnight."

"So?"

"And I need to get some sleep. So do you, by the way."

"Think you could sleep while I'm there?"

Another pause, but it feels different this time.

"You'd drive here in the middle of the night just to watch me sleep?"

The idea gives Alexander a very nice, warm, fuzzy feeling.

"I'd walk barefoot to Australia to watch you sleep."

Benjamin's laugh makes the warm fuzzy feeling even stronger.

"You're an idiot."

"So, you want an idiot tonight or not?"

Alexander is almost sure he's going to say no, but then he says yes. Very softly. Alexander can almost see the shy little glance. The one Benjamin does when he's afraid to get hurt but wants something bad enough to risk it anyway.

"On my way."


Benjamin opens the door in sweat-pants and a t-shirt, barefoot, his hair slightly tousled. Alexander thinks the guy has never looked this soft. And he's nervous. Alexander closes the door behind himself and pulls Benjamin into a hug. When he feels him relax Alexander gently says:

"Let's get you to bed."

Benjamin nods and pads into his bedroom. Alexander takes a breath and follows him. He hasn't been in that room since the day Benjamin moved in, and it didn't look much like a bedroom then. Now it feels and smells and looks like Benjamin all around, and it's incredibly intimate to even be there. Benjamin sits down on his bed.

"It's stupid to be this tense. It's just a job," he says, head bowed.


*The day he has to go back to school. Ninth grade, second try after five months in the clinic. Fear of fear. The thought of failing. Run away. Hide.*

Alexander studies Benjamin's posture.

"What's on your mind?"

Benjamin looks at him.

"I've never told you about the attacks."

Alexander squats down.

"Do you want to?"

Benjamin shakes his head.

"I just need you to know that I had them, back then, at fifteen. Panic attacks, unrest, anxiety. Cutting myself, the burns. Wasn't eating properly either. Spent five months in a psychology clinic."

He takes a deep breath.

"That's over now. It's behind me. And yet, right now, I feel exactly the way I did back then when I was supposed to go back to school."

"Your body remembers. It doesn't know yet that it's different this time, so it's falling back into old patterns."

Benjamin looks pensive. Alexander shrugs.

"Sorry. Trying to be a friend, but I can't always avoid going into therapist mode."

Benjamin gives him a grateful smile.

"Seems that's what I need tonight."

Alexander takes Benjamin's hands.

"You're nervous, that's to be expected. You'll do great once you get into it, but first days are always hard."

"I can't imagine Mr. Senne, psychotherapist, trembling like a leaf before his first day at the office."

"Oh you've got no idea."

Benjamin looks surprised.

"Can you tell me about it? No names, of course?"

"Only if you make yourself comfortable first."

Benjamin smiles at him and lays down on his side. Alexander hesitates for a moment but then he reaches out and pulls the blanket over Benjamin's shoulder. He feels a little silly, but only until he meets Benjamin's eyes. He's snuggling into the blanket, one corner tucked under his cheek. Alexander tries to find a more comfortable position on the floor.

"What are you doing down there? That's entirely too far away," Benjamin complains with a pout that should be illegal. Alexander looks at him, amused and a little insecure.

"Please?" Benjamin presses.

Alexander swallows.

"Benjamin Godan, are you trying to talk me into your bed?"

Benjamin makes puppy eyes at him and he gives in with a chuckle.

"You're impossible. You're lucky you're this hot."

Benjamin snuggles up to him, his back to Alexander's chest.

"You really think that?"

"You know I do."

Benjamin makes a tiny sound of surprised satisfaction. It's cute and heart-breaking at the same time. It's beyond Alexander why the guy would even remotely doubt his own attractiveness. He props himself up on one elbow and looks down at Benjamin.

"So, ready for your bed time story?"

The next morning Benjamin wakes up when his alarm goes off and immediately remembers what day it is. The fear is back. And then he remembers Alexander's voice lulling him to sleep. Alexander is gone, but his phone blinks. He reaches for it and sees three messages from Alexander — and two others — but he opens Alexander's first.

2:13 am: I'm back home. You're cute when you're asleep.

2:14 am: Actually, you're cute when you breathe. Hope you have sweet dreams.

6:02 am: So this is the big day! Go get them. You've got this. Let me know how it went. (Are phones allowed at school? Wink emoji.)

The other messages are from Chris and Angie. His study buddies are probably too excited about their own first days, and the fact that his father stays silent doesn't really come as a surprise. He closes his eyes for a moment.

"Hey Mum," he says very softly, "today's the day. I wish you were here to wish me luck. You'd probably say I don't need luck because I'm that good or something. Just keep an eye on me today, OK?"

Over his morning tea he texts Alexander:

Hey, I'm almost on my way. Feeling OK. Thank you for last night!

## Chapter 12

During lunch break Benjamin is too busy getting to know his colleagues and finding his way around to even look at his phone. By the time he leaves he's exhausted. Sitting in his car in the school's parking lot he tries to process the day's impressions, but it's just too much. He really wants to talk to Alexander, and Angie, and Chris, and above all he wants to know how everybody else was doing on their first day, but he realises there's no way he can handle all of that. *Just Alexander then*, he decides and turns his phone back on. *That's a lot of messages…* without reading any of them he just types:

Can I see you? and hits send. A few seconds later his phone rings. Alexander sounds worried.

"Are you OK?"

Benjamin lets his head fall back and exhales.

"Yeah, I guess I am. It's just — a lot to take in."

"Are you sure you want to come by? I won't be home for at least two hours, and you'd have to drive back later… unless… well, unless you wanna stay over, but then you'd have to drive back in the morning…"

"Just tell me if you don't want to see me," Benjamin says, and he's only half joking.

"Don't be an idiot."

"How about I come by your office? Just a quick hug between two appointments?"

He's trying very hard not to sound needy.

"Sure. Just knock."

"No way am I interrupting a session. I know you hate that."

"It's fine, Benjamin. Just let me know when you're there."


After seven years Benjamin is finally back at Alexander's office. It's a weird sensation, going there as a guest, a friend, or whatever it is that they are these days, instead of a patient. He takes a seat in the waiting area just like he has so many times, realising after a moment that he subconsciously chose his usual chair. He can't bring himself to knock on that door. This was a really bad idea. He gets up and walks towards the exit, his heart heavy and his throat closing up. He really wants to see Alexander, but he feels like he doesn't have any right to be there. To bother him at work. And then that door opens and Alexander looks at him with a soft, gentle smile that seems to melt his heart and heal his soul at the same time.

"Thought I heard something."

Benjamin avoids eye contact.

"Sorry."

Alexander takes three quick steps and reaches out for Benjamin.

"I said it's fine. It's OK for you to be here, Benjamin. Actually, I'm glad that you're here. I — missed you."

He looks at him, silently asking for permission, and Benjamin gives in. He opens his arms and Alexander steps that tiny bit closer. They hug, holding on to each other for a precious moment, and before they part, Alexander brushes a tiny kiss against Benjamin's neck.

"I gotta go back in there," Alexander murmurs.

Benjamin nods.

"Thank you," he says with a small smile. "Call me later? If you have a little time?"

"Will do."


They talk about their respective days almost every night of that week.

On Friday morning before leaving the house Benjamin texts:

I'd really like to see you soon. Are you free some time over the weekend?

A: I'll be working kinda late tonight and I have a conference tomorrow.

B: Oh, so I guess you'll want a little peace and quiet on Sunday.

A: I do, but I wouldn't mind having peace and quiet with *you*.

Benjamin's screen is a little blurry for a moment.

A: Conference is scheduled to end at 4 o'clock. Wanna come by my place say, at 6? I'll cook.

B: You don't have to cook after an exhausting day. I can get something.

A: It's fine. I want to. You could help if you like.

Benjamin smiles at the idea of cooking with Alexander. He's not much of a cook himself but working together sounds nice. Domestic.

B: Cool. I'm in. I'll bring a bottle.

There's a long silence, and Benjamin gets ready to leave for work when his phone beeps one more time.

A: Wanna stay over?


Mr. Godan is a little distracted during that school day. Does he want to stay at Alexander's? He pulls himself together after the third spelling error in a row. The kids are having a blast, but there's only so many times he can pull the old 'just checking if you're paying attention' stunt. When the last class of the day is over, he stays put and pulls out his phone. One message from Alexander:

Sorry if that was too blunt or too sudden. We can just have dinner, maybe watch a movie, no problem.

Sent three hours after the other one. He must have kept thinking about it… Benjamin feels more than just a little guilty. He hits call after taking a deep breath. But of course Alexander's still working and doesn't answer his phone.

"Hey, it's me. Sorry… I guess I had some thinking to do. I'd really like to stay over. Hope you didn't worry or anything… you're not mad at me, are you?"

He puts his phone in his back pocket and closes his eyes, heart beating a little faster. That's it. He said yes.


A few hours later Benjamin's phone rings. It takes him a moment to pick up.

"Hey," Alexander says.

"Hey! You sound a little tired."

"I am. Long day. Anyway. What'cha doing?"

Benjamin grins.

"Actually, I'm taking a bath."

There's a pause.

"You're doing this on purpose."

Benjamin chuckles.

"Well, it *was* kind of intentional — not like I fell into the tub or anything."

Now Alexander is laughing, too. Benjamin likes the sound, warm and rich and already less stressed. And then Alexander clears his throat.

"Look, about those last messages."

Benjamin stops smiling.

"Yeah?"

"I — it kind of bugs me that I don't know — "

He sighs.

"Ah crap, we shouldn't be doing this over the phone."

"Doing what?"

"Never mind. Are you really OK with staying at my place?"

"Well, I don't have to, if you'd rather, you know—"

There's an awkward silence on both ends. Alexander takes a breath. His voice is very gentle and deliberate:

"I miss you, Benjamin. It's nice to hear your voice but at the same time I wish you were here. That I could look at you. Be close to you. I'd really like to have that tomorrow. But I'm not sure if that's what you want and I guess I'm just scared… Jesus. The fact that you're naked doesn't help at all right now," he says, and Benjamin can hear the grin slipping into his voice. They both start laughing again. Benjamin catches himself first.

"Listen, I'd love to spend some time with you. There's so much I'd like to tell you. Why don't you do your conference tomorrow—I have quite a lot of work myself, actually—and then we'll have a nice dinner together and just—see where it leads, OK?"

"OK."

"So I'll be there at six then."

"Can't wait. Sleep well."

"You too."

Benjamin puts his phone away and exhales, a warm, happy smile spreading on his face.

# Chapter 13

Benjamin tries really hard to get everything done the next day. He can't help but think about the evening though. And the night, possibly. It's been a while since he's done anything more than a little making out on a dance floor. And Alexander is special. He catches himself trying to recall the way he felt about the older man back then. A crush, for sure. Some form of hero worship, maybe. Now it's different. Like they're on the same level. More or less. They're still a few years apart obviously, but it doesn't feel like a lot. Benjamin starts to smile. He's really looking forward to seeing Alexander, despite being nervous and a little insecure.

By the time he rings Alexander's door-bell he's very nervous and very insecure. And it all just vanishes the moment Alexander opens the door and smiles at him like he's the best thing Alexander has seen all week.

"Hey," Alexander greats him, and they hug briefly, but closely.

Benjamin drops his over-night bag and shrugs out of his leather jacket. Alexander takes it from him and hangs it up.

"Want me to give you the tour?"

"Sure!"

They finish the tour in the kitchen, and Benjamin is put to good use, chopping vegetables and preparing a salad while Alexander makes Bolognese. They've opened the wine Benjamin brought and are talking about their respective weeks as they go, and then everything is ready and they sit down at the table Alexander has already set.

"This is delicious, Alexander."

"Thanks. I like to think of pasta as comfort food."

"And you thought I needed comfort?"

He takes as sip of his wine and looks at Alexander over the rim of the glass. Alexander plays with his fork, not looking up.

"I thought I might need it."

When he does look up Benjamin's eyebrows are raised in a silent question.

"You're making me nervous. This, us, it's making me nervous."

"That's OK," Benjamin says with a smile, "me too."

They eat in silence for a little while, glancing at each other every now and then. Eventually Benjamin starts talking about his students, how he's desperate to get all the names right as quickly as possible.

"I drew sketches of the class-room and put the names to the seats. And I know I shouldn't have favourites but there's this one boy who reminds me so much of myself, I can't help but like him."

"What's he like?" Alexander asks, and they both know it's actually, 'What were you like when you were his age?'

"Smart, but shy. Always worried he might say something wrong, but when you get him to talk he's usually right."

Benjamin plays with his glass.

"You know, I have this idea… remember my Henry adaptation?"

"Sure I do!"

"I'd like to do a theatre project based on that. And young Florian would be the perfect Prince Hal. And then there's Jenny. We talked about what everybody wanted to be when they grow up and she said she wanted to study psychology. She's smart, but she's a teenager, so school isn't really high on her agenda and she's a little lazy I think."

"Want me to talk to her?" Alexander asks with a grin.

"I thought of that to be honest. During orientation week maybe? She could use a little talk, you know, how her grades need to be first class to be able to study and stuff? And please do tell her what an amazing profession it is."

"Ya think?"

"I do. And you're good."

Alexander blushes a little.

"Anyway. Wanna tell me about that conference?"

Alexander starts talking, a bit hesitant at first, but after a while he gets more and more excited, and Benjamin thinks his enthusiasm is irresistible. He starts losing himself in Alexander's voice, the way his eyes sparkle and his hands move, until Alexander suddenly stops talking. A smile is spreading on his face while he slightly cocks his head.

"Sorry. Got carried away I'm afraid."

Benjamin pushes his chair back and walks around the table. He takes Alexander's hand.

"Me too," he whispers and traces Alexander's jawline with his fingertips, and then he leans in for a soft, slow kiss. Alexander responds to it, and they end up on the couch without really knowing how they got there.

"There was going to be dessert," Alexander murmurs after a while.

"Would that involve one of us getting up from the couch?"

"Well, yeah, I'm afraid so."

"That's a very silly idea."

They settle in, cuddled up to each other. They don't talk much but kiss a lot, gentle touches here and there, and every now and then they just look at each other.

"How about we get a little more comfortable?" Benjamin finally asks with an expression that is equal parts mischief and insecurity. Alexander's heart skips a beat, but then he nods.

"I like the sound of that."

He gets up, and Benjamin follows his example.

In the bedroom they start kissing again, and it quickly gets more and more passionate. Alexander's hands wander beneath Benjamin's tee, and when Alexander sees permission in his eyes, he pulls it over Benjamin's head.

Benjamin unbuttons Alexander's shirt and slips it over his shoulders, and then he lays down on the bed and looks up at Alexander. Alexander sits down and looks at Benjamin for a long time.

"You've put on some muscle."

"Some weight training instead of just running," Benjamin says and shrugs.

*New image. Too many older guys with a thing for twinks, and not a single one of them even the slightest bit attractive.*

And then Benjamin realises that back then Alexander seemed to have liked that, too. He bites his lip.

"Is that a bad thing?"

Alexander stares at him.

"Well…" Benjamin shrugs his shoulders.

"You've got to be kidding me! You, my dear, are the type of man guys like me always just adore from afar — or put in their lockers — but never get."

He tries very hard not to glance down at his own — certainly not overweight, but untrained — body.

"There was a time when the good-looking guys were jerks, and us average guys had a chance by being decent. But if there are smart, handsome men now who also are decent people…"

Benjamin explodes with laughter.

"You're an idiot," he whispers and pulls Alexander close, both arms wrapped around his torso. When Alexander starts to relax, Benjamin rolls them over and presses small gentle kisses to Alexander's cheekbones, his neck and chest. When Benjamin's lips brush his stomach, Alexander's head falls back with a moan. And then Alexander feels gentle pressure and warm breath through his jeans — and freezes.

*A much younger Benjamin is sitting across the desk from him at the practice, shaken, vulnerable — and Alexander wants to touch him so badly. His fingernails dig into his palms. He's punishing himself, forbids himself that longing. What he feels is wrong. Forbidden, and rightly so. Benjamin trusts him. What's going on in Alexander's head is abuse.*

Benjamin pulls back. Alexander's jaw is clenched.

"Are you OK? Did I do something wrong?"

Alexander forces his muscles to relax.

"No. It's — I'm sorry. I'm an idiot."

Benjamin lays down next to him and looks at him.

"Talk to me. Are you having second thoughts? Is this too much too soon? Too fast?"

Alexander turns and rests his forehead against Benjamin's.

"I can't do this. I'm so sorry, but I can't."

Benjamin swallows and turns away.

"I see. That's — it's fine. I'm sorry. I guess I'd better leave."

Alexander is frozen in place. He watches Benjamin turn his back towards him and put his tee back on. Any minute now he's going to leave, and who knows if he'll ever feel like coming back. Alexander stares at him, caught up in a memory that's still painful after all that time.

*Christian, leaving, pissed because Alexander isn't in the mood. Disappearing into town to find someone for the night. Telling Alexander he doesn't mind if he does the same. Unwilling to understand that Alexander doesn't want that. That he wants nothing more than to be held. For Christian to be with him even if he doesn't 'function.' Their last fight. Christian accusing Alexander of smothering him.*

*Please don't. Please don't leave*, Alexander thinks desperately, but he doesn't say it. It didn't do any good back then. It won't now.

Benjamin pauses in the bedroom door, insecure, hesitant. His fingertips brush the door handle.

"What did I do wrong?"

Alexander can't get up fast enough. He frames Benjamin's face with both hands and kisses him, long and hungrily.

"Nothing, Benjamin, nothing at all. It's me. Please don't go. I don't want to lose you."

Benjamin takes his hand and leads him back to the bed.

"Tell me," he says and sits down. Alexander plops down next to him.

"It's stupid."

"Possible. Tell me anyway."

"It's all me. You're amazing, and hot, and I want you so bad I can hardly think straight, but – there's stuff we need to talk about. I thought it was OK, that I was over it, but I can't stop thinking about it."

"About what?"

"About the way I felt back then, when you were my patient. The way I'd look at you sometimes, when you weren't looking. The way I felt about you. The things I dreamed about. None of that was OK, it was completely inappropriate! There are very good reasons why therapists aren't allowed to get involved with their patients. And now, I'm here with you, in my bedroom, in my bed, and I feel like a freaking pervert."

He runs his hand through his hair and tries to get his voice under control. His hands are shaking.

"Even though you're not my patient any more – given all the things you told me back then I feel as if I tricked you into giving in, agreeing… whatever. I'm sorry, Benjamin. I'm so sorry."

Benjamin lets out a breath.

"You do realise this isn't very rational."

Alexander chuckles.

"I do. Maybe I need counselling."

"Maybe you need a priest," Benjamin says and rolls his eyes.

Alexander goes very still, and then he sits up and kisses Benjamin.

"You're brilliant."

"I am?"

"I think I'll go to church tomorrow. See a man about a guy."

"I'm not really following you, but whatever floats your boat."

Alexander lays back and looks up at Benjamin.

"Would you consider me very weird if I asked you to stay with me tonight?"

# Chapter 14

Alexander leaves the church after service, making sure he's the last person to shake the pastor's hand. The grey-haired man holds on to Alexander's hand for that tiny moment longer.

"Alexander! I haven't seen you in a long time. How are you?"

"I'm here because I'd like to talk to you."

Pastor Arnim looks at him with a warm smile and nods.

"Coffee, then?"

"Yes, please."

They walk side by side in silence. A few minutes later they are sitting in the pastor's homely kitchen, and Alexander stares into his mug trying to find the right words.

"You wanna start with small talk or rather tell me right away why you're here?"

Alexander smiles gratefully and relaxes a little.

"There was this young man I was working with, and after a while I realised that I was… falling for him."

Alexander sighs and rubs his face.

"I caught myself looking at him, thinking of him in ways I shouldn't have."

Very cautiously the pastor asks:

"Did you ever *do* anything inappropriate or unethical?"

"Not… well, no. I ended it."

"Which was the right thing to do. Did you explain it to him?"

"Yes. He didn't take it so well. But eventually, he understood."

"You stayed in contact?"

Alexander blushes.

"Actually—we recently ran into each other and—now we're dating. Or whatever you wanna call it. We talk on the phone, we spend time together, and it's good! I like being with him, I like *him*, a lot, and on the one hand I'm happier than I've been in a long time. But on the other hand this whole thing feels so wrong! I'm scared someone might ask how we met because it'll make me look like a pervert. Like a paedophile."

The pastor raises his eyebrows. Alexander feels like he has to clarify:

"He was twenty-one when we met, but he was younger than his years. Good Lord, he was little more than a kid. How could I look at that kid and start having those feelings for him? He was amazing—smart and beautiful—and he had been through so much and left it all behind him, like a phoenix from the ashes… and I would look at him like—prey."

The pastor takes a deep breath and puts his hand on Alexander's arm.

"He wasn't a kid. And you didn't do anything wrong, Alexander. To me it sounds like you saw a very special person you were falling in love with."

Arnim gives him a moment, then he straightens.

"When you met again, who made the first move?"

Alexander thinks back and starts to smile.

"Thank you."

"You're welcome."

"Now for the small talk…"


Alexander is sitting in his car, pondering the conversation he had with pastor Arnim, and all of a sudden he longs for Benjamin so badly it's almost unbearable. He pulls his phone from his pocket and calls him.

"Hey," Benjamin says, "how did it go?"

"Can I see you?"

Benjamin laughs softly.

"Sure. Come over."

There are butterflies in Alexander's stomach when he hangs up.


The butterflies are going crazy when he arrives at Benjamin's—who's already waiting, leaning against the door.

"Hey," Alexander says with a broad, happy smile.

"Hey," Benjamin answers and steps back to let Alexander in. "You're beaming! Seems like it worked."

Alexander pulls the door closed and looks straight at Benjamin. For a moment it seems like Alexander is about to say something, but then he just kisses Benjamin.

"Wow," Benjamin says with a grin. "I don't know what the pastor told you, but I like the guy."

Alexander starts laughing, relieved and happy, and kisses him again.

"If you keep this up," Benjamin whispers right into Alexander's ear, "you're going to end up in my bed very soon."

"I wouldn't say no to that."

Benjamin pulls back enough to meet Alexander's eyes.

"Are you sure?"

Alexander just nods. It makes Benjamin's eyes sparkle.

"Come on," he says softly and takes Alexander's hand.


They are lying in bed, facing each other, and Benjamin is very serious.

"I'm not your patient any more, I'm an adult, and I know what I want. What do *you* want? Right now?"

Alexander hesitates for a moment, but then he pulls himself together.

"I want to kiss you. Not just your lips. Your whole body. I want to find out what you like, what turns you on. I want you to enjoy and let go. I'll do anything you want, Benjamin."

Benjamin chuckles.

"Sounds like I won the lottery."

Alexander grins.

"You're worth it."

He turns serious.

"OK — so what do *you* want?"

Benjamin props himself up on his elbow and looks down at Alexander.

"I want you to feel me."

Alexander swallows and looks up at him. Benjamin locks eyes and rolls on top of him, making him feel the full weight of his body. Alexander's eyes close. Benjamin kisses his neck.

"I want you to see the man I've become, not the kid I used to be. I want you beneath me. I want you to feel how much I want you. How badly you turn me on."

Alexander moans. His hands wander across Benjamin's back to his waist. He pulls him close, presses his body to Benjamin's, and then he relaxes into the mattress and enjoys the weight of Benjamin's slender, muscular body.

"You like being dominant."

"Does that surprise you?"

"It does, to be honest."

Alexander thinks back to the fantasies he used to have. *Huh. Interesting.* Benjamin shrugs.

"It depends. But generally—yeah, I like being in control."

Alexander bites his lip, but he can't quite suppress the little moan far back in his throat.

"You're perfect," he breathes. "How do I deserve you?"

"You don't—not yet," Benjamin says, and the tone of his voice stirs something in Alexander, "but I'm sure you'll think of something…"

# Chapter 15

From then on Alexander is more comfortable around Benjamin, more relaxed, and they spend more and more time together. Personal belongings are left at each other's places – and spare keys are exchanged. One day Alexander is sitting on Benjamin's couch while Benjamin is still at work. They want to cook dinner together later. Alexander is looking for something to pass the time and comes across that Brahms-CD again. He can't resist. Head resting against the wall and eyes closed he listens. And then, without really knowing why, he looks up – and freezes. It's impossible to tell how long Benjamin has been standing there. Alexander pauses the music.

"I'm sorry," he says.

"It's OK."

Benjamin's voice is absolutely toneless, without any emotion. It scares the shit out of Alexander. He gets up and walks towards Benjamin, slowly, carefully, the way one approaches a shy animal.

"I know what this music means to you. I should have stayed away from it."

Benjamin doesn't say a word.

"Say something, please!"

Benjamin walks past him and starts the music again. He's standing with his back towards Alexander, completely motionless.

"I wanted—I was trying to get to know her, but I had no right. I'm so sorry. We should turn it off."

"No," Benjamin says. "I want to listen to it. I've been wanting to listen to it for years but I was too scared."

Alexander steps close. Benjamin leans against him, relaxing the slightest bit.

"With you by my side I might be able to do it," he whispers. Alexander's throat goes dry. He wraps his arms around Benjamin and pulls him close.

"...as one whom his own mother comforteth..."

Alexander closes his eyes. He doesn't even want to imagine what Benjamin must feel like.

"Come here," he breathes and puts his hands on Benjamin's shoulders. Benjamin turns around and melts into Alexander's arms, and then he loses it. His whole body is shaking, and the more he fights it the worse it gets.

"It's all right. It's OK to cry. I'm here."

"It's been years! I should be over it by now!"

Alexander rubs his back.

"She was your mother, and you loved her."

Tears are running down Benjamin's cheeks and his breathing is irregular. Alexander looks at him, kisses him and pulls him back into a hug.

"I miss her so much," Benjamin whispers.

He sounds utterly spent.

"I know. Do you want to talk about her?"

Benjamin shakes his head.

"OK."

Alexander sits back down on the couch and looks at Benjamin. Benjamin hesitates for a moment, but then he lays down, his head in Alexander's lap. They listen to the rest of the requiem without talking. Alexander strokes Benjamin's hair, and eventually Benjamin calms down.

After the last chord Benjamin says:

"I know who my birth mother was by the way."

Alexander straightens.

"You found her?"

"I found out *about* her."

"Really? When?"

"Almost a year ago."

"Huh. When we talked about her in therapy you told me you didn't care who she was, that you never tried to find her, but I wasn't sure if that was the truth."

"It was. I didn't care. But recently I started thinking about it more and more. So I tried to find out who she was. Why she didn't want me."

Alexander carefully studies him.

"So what did you find?"

"She was only 17 when I was born. The name she gave the hospital was most probably not her real name, and two days after I was born she vanished. She just left me there. She didn't tell anyone who my father was, maybe she didn't even know his name herself."

Benjamin takes a deep breath.

"Anyway, I realised that the life my parents gave me, my adoptive parents I mean, wasn't so bad. Even if it was far from being perfect, they still took care of me and provided me with everything I needed. I could have had a much worse childhood, or probably have died as a baby, if she'd kept me. She just couldn't take care of a kid."

"Do you regret looking for her?"

Benjamin shakes his head and sits up.

"No. I think I needed it. Back then I couldn't have handled it. When you asked me about it I really didn't care. Couldn't let myself care. But now I'm glad I know these things."

Alexander just looks at him, silently asking for a kiss, and Benjamin complies. When their lips part, their foreheads touch.

"I love you," Benjamin says very softly, his eyes closed and a gentle smile on his face, "you're amazing. You make me feel special, and safe. I love you."

Alexander just stares at him, and then he starts to smile, a wide, joyful smile that makes his eyes sparkle.

"I love *you*," he responds, and there's something like wonder in his voice. He's overwhelmed, almost speechless. He repeats it, trying the words out. Getting used to saying them out loud after all those times he's just thought them. Benjamin kisses him again, and then they just hold each other for an eternity, revelling in warmth and tenderness. They fall asleep much later that night and wake up in each other's arms, and they can't be bothered to get out of bed until way past noon.

# Chapter 16

One night when Alexander returns from a conference quite exhausted, he finds a note on the floor of his apartment:

Don't be alarmed. I'm in your bed (and probably already asleep). Ben.

*That can't be true.* Alexander feels like shouting his happiness into the night shy. He hurries to the bathroom, trying to be as quiet as possible, and then he carefully opens the bedroom door. What a sight. The street-light in front of his house shines on a sleeping Benjamin, and Alexander can't remember seeing anything more beautiful in his life. He slips under the blanket with a happy smile. On the one hand he hopes for Benjamin to wake up and look at him, but on the other hand he doesn't want to disturb his sleep. Benjamin doesn't move. *Just as well.* Alexander lays on his side and simply looks at him. And then he very carefully moves closer. Benjamin wakes up enough to notice Alexander, but not enough to say anything. His eyes close again and he cuddles up to Alexander with a content little smile. Alexander feels like he's about to burst with joy.

"I love you," he whispers and kisses Benjamin's temple. One arm around Benjamin he falls asleep.

The next morning Benjamin wakes up first. When Alexander opens his eyes Benjamin is smiling at him.

"Hey."

"Hey." Alexander stretches his body. "How did I deserve this surprise?"

"You sounded stressed out on the phone, so I felt like doing something nice for you. Cheer you up. When I finally lay here in bed on my own I wasn't so sure if it had been a good idea. I mean maybe you wanted to be left alone..."

Alexander pulls him into his arms.

"I'm so happy you're here. Coming home to *you* — that feels so incredibly good."

For a while they just lay there, holding each other, but then Benjamin starts getting restless. Alexander grins. *The guy just can't keep still.*

"OK, what would you normally do on a Saturday morning?"

"Run, I guess."

"Did you bring your running shoes?"

"I did."

It sounds as if he's a bit embarrassed to admit that.

"Is that OK?"

"Of course it's OK! Here's an idea: you go for a run, I make breakfast. How much time do I have?"

"Until I'm back and showered? Ninety minutes maybe?"

Alexander hugs his pillow.

"Great. So I can stay put for a little while longer."

Benjamin chuckles and gets out of bed.

"But don't go back to sleep or I'll starve to death!"

Alexander grins.

"Get lost."

Benjamin bows down and kisses his forehead.

"Sleepyhead."

Alexander growls at him, but he's still smiling.


When Benjamin returns a good hour later Alexander has crisped up bread rolls, set the table, pressed out oranges, made coffee and put bacon and eggs on the stove. Benjamin stops in the kitchen door and tries to pick his jaw off the floor.

"That isn't breakfast, that's a feast!"

Alexander turns around with a grin.

"Can't have you starving!"

He turns his attention back to the frying pan. Benjamin stands close, his hands on Alexander's waist.

"You're gorgeous," he murmurs and kisses the back of Alexander's neck. "Be right back."


He showers in record time. Alexander is just putting bacon and eggs on the table when he shows up in the kitchen again, hair still a little damp. Alexander stills and looks at him.

"What?"

"You're too good to be true."

Benjamin blushes a little. Alexander puts the plate down and steps close.

"And you smell good," he murmurs and kisses Benjamin's neck. His hands wander over Benjamin's shoulders and his back. Benjamin puts his arms around Alexander's waist, closes his eyes and enjoys Alexander's touch. And then his stomach rumbles. Alexander bursts out laughing and steps back. He pulls Benjamin's chair out and waits for him to sit. Then he bends down, both hands on Benjamin's shoulders.

"I probably shouldn't say it, but I love spoiling you."

Benjamin's head falls back and he looks at Alexander.

"I could get used to it."

"Exactly," Alexander says with a grin and takes his seat.


After breakfast Benjamin insists on cleaning up the kitchen.

"Knock yourself out. That's my least favourite part anyway."

Alexander gets up and stretches.

"I'll have to spend two, maybe three hours at the practice. Do you want to stay until I'm back?"

"I have quite a lot of exercise books to mark, but I can do it here if you don't mind. Brought everything."

Once more Alexander gets the impression that Benjamin is a little embarrassed.

"I like that you've planned ahead. It's good to know you like being here. Feels nice."

Alexander hugs him.

"That way I can come home to you *again*. I like that a lot."

It takes Alexander a while to leave the house, but then he makes his way to his practice with a new spring in his step — and Benjamin covers the dining room table in his students' exercise books.

# Chapter 17

"How would you feel about meeting my parents?" Alexander asks casually one day while they're watching a movie at Benjamin's place. Benjamin doesn't react. Alexander kisses Benjamin's shoulder and rests his chin on it.

"No opinion on the subject?"

"You told your parents about us? When?"

"A while ago."

Benjamin shrugs off Alexander's touch.

"I thought it was obvious that I don't want that."

"Ben, please, it's —"

Benjamin jumps up, unable to sit still any longer, and gets himself a beer. He doesn't ask if Alexander wants one too. Alexander's head falls back against the backrest. He lets out a breath. *Drama queen.* When Benjamin refuses to sit back down Alexander gets up as well.

"Can we please have a civil discussion about this?"

Benjamin doesn't react. He's leaning against the kitchen door and refuses to look at Alexander. "Ben?"

Now he does look at him, but Alexander almost wishes he hadn't. Alexander can't keep up that eye contact. Benjamin's voice is very quiet, but it cuts like a knife:

"You *know* I don't want to come out. Not yet. And most definitely I don't want anybody *else* to out me, especially not without my knowledge! What were you thinking? Did you mean to present me with a fait accompli? Do you think you're *helping*? Or were you just fed up waiting?"

*Different kitchen, same discussion. Julian giving him an ultimatum, unwilling to wait any longer. Panic.*

*"You said you were OK with it. You said you wouldn't pressure me!"*

*"How much longer, Ben? How much longer do you want to hide? I'm sick of lying or being scared I might say something wrong. I'm sick of wondering if I can smile at you, or how close I can stand, or if I can touch you. I can't take this much longer!"*

*Over and over they have that conversation until Julian finally gives up — and leaves him. It's painful, for both of them, and Benjamin blames himself for the breakup. He used to be happy with Julian, but that wasn't enough.*

"I didn't out you, for fuck's sake. Would you just listen to me?"

"You told your parents about me. Told them we were dating. How is that not outing?"

Alexander takes a deep breath.

"Ben. Please. Please calm down and let me explain. I love you. I'd never do anything I *know* you don't want."

Benjamin says nothing, but the look in his eyes softens. He's waiting.

"I told them I met someone, but they don't know who you are. No name, nothing. I just told them there's someone in my life—and that I'm very happy with that someone."

Benjamin is still looking at him, the beginning of a smile in his eyes. Alexander sighs. With a good humoured eye roll he continues:

"So, my parents being my parents, they asked if they could meet the man who makes me happy. I told them it's not that easy. I said I'd talk to you, and that it's your decision. And it is, Ben. If you don't want it that's fine. I won't put any pressure on you. Never. OK?"

Benjamin's shoulders drop and he looks down.

"I'm an idiot, aren't I?"

"Sometimes. But you're *my* idiot."

Benjamin doesn't bite.

"I guess I'm just scared. Like—that makes it kinda official."

"Like you can't pull out after that?"

"No! I mean—I don't want to pull out! I love you. I want to be with you. I *want* to tell people. I'm just too much of a coward I guess."

Alexander closes the distance between them. Benjamin looks up, confused and exhausted. Alexander kisses him gently, and finally Benjamin relaxes a little.

"Look, one doesn't necessarily have anything to do with the other. We could have dinner with my parents without you officially coming out. They just want to meet you. They don't have to talk about it if you don't want them to."

"Ya think they'd be OK with that?"

"Sure! They just want you to know that you're welcome. It doesn't have to be next week. Would you just give it some thought please?"

# Chapter 18

Benjamin gives it a lot of thought, and finally he says yes. On their way to Alexander's parents' house he's very quiet.

*In Benjamin's head layer after layer of memories and emotions merge into a solid crust of tension, humiliation, fury, helplessness and fear.*

*His mother, looking forward to "all her men" sitting around the dining room table. His father's phone call, saying he won't be able to make it. Benjamin's relief when his mother removes the redundant plate. His guilt as he notices her disappointment.*

*Other occasions when his father is present. Little Benjamin trying to draw his father's attention to himself, away from Chris. Being scolded for interrupting his brother. His attempts at joining in on his father's and big brother's conversation. His resignation when he realises that his father just won't listen to him. That he's just not interested in what Benjamin has to say.*

*Young Benjamin giving up and remaining silent during dinner, his eyes on his plate whenever his father is present; missing his father's prompt because he's daydreaming. And time and again, his relief at being allowed to leave the table. Every single time.*

And then they are standing on the steps leading to Alexander's parents' front door, and Benjamin is very pale. Alexander takes his hand for a moment and looks him in the eyes.

"You can do this. I'm there. Remember the secret escape plan?"

Benjamin chuckles.

"I don't want to escape. It's all right, I'm good."

Alexander gives him a wide smile.

"Ready then?"

"Ready."

Alexander unlocks the door and calls:

"Mum? Dad? We're here!"

From somewhere in the house a woman's voice calls back:

"I'm almost finished, Alexander! Meanwhile, why don't you go to the living room?"

Alexander grins.

"Typical. Come on."

They sit down on the couch, but Benjamin can't sit still for more than two seconds. Alexander opens the sliding door leading to the terrace, and they step outside.

"This is amazing," Benjamin says when he sees the garden. He takes a few steps onto the terrace and looks out over the lawn, flowers and trees.

"You like it?" Alexander asks softly, standing behind Benjamin. Benjamin leans back against his chest.

"I love it. My parents never cared much for a garden, so we basically had a lawn. Dad and Chris would throw balls and stuff, but there wasn't much there for me. This is gorgeous. I'd sit and read for hours if I had a place like this."

Alexander can picture it in his mind. It's a beautiful image. *Maybe one day…* he gently squeezes Benjamin's waist before letting go and turning around.

"Hey Mum," he says and hugs her.

"Hey Alexander," she says with affection and holds him for a moment. Then she lets go and turns towards Benjamin.

"And this must be Benjamin."

She shakes his hand with a smile.

"Welcome to our house."

"Thank you, Mrs Senne. Or do you prefer Dr Senne?"

Her smile widens.

"Rahel is fine. Otherwise there will be confusion in this house."

Benjamin returns her smile and nods.

"Rahel. That's an unusual name."

She nods.

"Biblical, like yours. But I'm sure you know that."


*Benjamin's mother saying his name. Soft and lovingly. Her youngest. The little one. So much more her son than her husband's. And in actual fact – neither.*

Benjamin pulls himself together. Rahel Senne turns towards Alexander:

"Your father is late as always," she says with a good-humoured eye roll that Benjamin thinks looks familiar.

They sit down at the dinner table and decide to start without Alexander's father. Every now and then Alexander touches Benjamin or smiles at him, and Benjamin starts to relax. Rahel is friendly and open, asks him about his job and listens with interest. When she hears that Benjamin likes theatre she gives her son a look.

"What?!"

Rahel grins.

"Maybe *you* can interest my low-brow son in it. I gave it up."

"Mum!"

Benjamin starts to grin, too. And then his expression softens.

"We could all go together. I'll find something you'll like."

Benjamin has a hard time analysing the look in Alexander's eyes. Rahel likes the idea.


When mother and son are alone in the kitchen for a moment Rahel winks at Alexander.

"You look happy."

Alexander's smile speaks volumes.

"I like him, Alex. You're both welcome in this house any time you want."

Alexander quickly hugs his mother and they leave the kitchen together.


A moment later there's the sound of a key turning in the front door. Alexander and his mother look at each other. Neither one of them notices that Benjamin freezes. Dr Senne enters the dining room, gives everybody a confused look, and then it dawns on him.

"Oh my god, Rahel, I forgot!"

"You've got to be kidding me."

He extends his hand to Benjamin.

"Benjamin! I'm so sorry, please forgive me! Alexander brings home an important guest and I…"

Benjamin swallows, shakes Alexander's father's hand and clears his throat.

"That's no problem, I'm sure you were very busy."

Ulrich Senne bites his lip.

"I was, it wasn't anything I couldn't have done tomorrow though. I just didn't remember!"

Alexander chuckles and shakes his head, getting up to greet his father.

"We thought you were busy saving a life."

"Can I leave and enter again and we'll pretend it was like that?"

He looks contrite. His wife grins.

"You can make dessert—in compensation. But for now just sit down, there's plenty left."

Benjamin reaches for Alexander's hand under the table. Alexander looks at him quizzically and brushes his thumb over the back of Benjamin's hand, but Benjamin is stone-still. Alexander clears his throat.

"I'll have to borrow the guest for a moment," he says lightly and stands.


A minute later they are standing in Alexander's former room which is the guest room now, and Alexander wraps his arms around Benjamin. Very slowly Benjamin starts to relax. Eventually he says with a sigh:

"I'm sorry. It's OK now. Let's not make them wait any longer."

Alexander frames his face with both hands and looks at him. Benjamin avoids his gaze.

"Ben. Hey, look at me."

Benjamin's gaze wanders. Alexander waits until he finally looks at him.

"What can I do?"

Benjamin shrugs his shoulders.

"I don't even know myself. Guess I'll just have to deal with it."

Alexander sighs and enfolds him in an embrace again, not at all happy with that answer—but he knows it's all he'll get right now.

"Do you want to leave?"

The short moment it takes Benjamin to say no speaks volumes.

"That's fine, if this is too much for you—"

"It's just dinner for fuck's sake!"

Benjamin frees himself. For a moment his outburst hangs in the air between them, and then Benjamin takes a deep breath.

"I'm sorry."

He takes Alexander's hand.

"Let's go back."

"Are you sure?"

Benjamin nods, and they go back, holding hands.


When they enter the dining room Rahel is clearing the table. Benjamin hurries to help. She's about to say something when she catches Alexander's look. He shakes his head very slightly, and she swallows it.

"Where's Dad?"

"In the kitchen. Compensation."

Alexander beams.

"Oh cool, that means Kaiserschmarrn!"

"Exactly."

Benjamin looks at him quizzically.

"My dad's Kaiserschmarrn is legendary. Takes forever, but totally worth the wait."

They sit back down, and Rahel refills Benjamin's wine glass.

"Alexander?"

"No thanks, I'm driving."

"You could stay, the guest room is ready."

Benjamin looks at Alexander who smiles at him reassuringly.

"It's fine, I'll stick with water."


When Ulrich Senne finally steps out of the kitchen with a huge heap of Kaiserschmarrn everybody digs in enthusiastically. Benjamin's plate is empty in record time. Alexander's father is flattered and asks if he'd like a second serving.

"I'd love to! This is really, really good."

Alexander grins and pushes back his own plate.

"If I ran ten kilometres per day I could afford to eat like that, too."

"Three times a week tops."

"Wow," Ulrich Senne comments, "that's ambitious. I wouldn't have that kind of discipline."

"I never really liked sports as a kid, but then I discovered running, and it feels good. Frees my mind. I just don't get enough exercise during the day."

Alexander looks back and forth between his father and Benjamin and then at his mother. She's looking content. Alexander feels a tension leave his body that he hadn't been aware of. A warm, fuzzy feeling starts spreading in his belly. The people he loves most in the world are seated at this table. Life is good.


In the car on their way back home Benjamin clears his throat.

"Are you disappointed because I didn't wanna stay?"

"It's fine. I get it. We don't have to do everything at once."

Benjamin lets out a small sigh of relief.

"It was very kind of them to offer, though. Some other time I'd really like to do it."

Benjamin smiles.

"They like you a lot."

"I like them, too. You resemble your mother very much." Alexander checks the rear-view mirror and glances at Benjamin before turning his attention back to the road. Benjamin chuckles.

"You have her eyes, but that's not what I meant."

He puts his hand on Alexander's thigh.

"The same quiet, friendly strength. The ability to create trust. I thought that was a result of your job, but it's probably the other way around. You're that good at your job because you have that."

Alexander swallows. Benjamin leans back in his seat.

"Must have been nice, growing up in that house. In a family like that."

"It was. Is it—difficult? For you? Experiencing that?"

Benjamin thinks about it for a moment, and then he shakes his head.

"No, actually I'm happy you have that. And that I get to be a part of it now."

Alexander is very quiet for a long while after that. When he finds his voice it's to simply say:

"I love you."

# Chapter 19

One night Alexander wakes up because Benjamin is restless beside him, and when he sees the tension on Benjamin's face he gently tries to wake him up. It takes a long time for Benjamin to surface from whatever it is he's dreaming about. When he does, he looks exhausted and upset and doesn't want to talk about it.

"It's always the same thing." That's all he says, but he silently asks to be held, and of course Alexander does. Benjamin goes back to sleep, but Alexander lies awake for a long time afterwards.

Over the next weeks Benjamin works on making his Henry stage play happen and it's pretty much all he talks about. Alexander loves how enthusiastic he is even though he suspects the workload might actually be a bit much. He makes Benjamin promise to spend a weekend away when everything is over and otherwise supports him where he can. It means that they see each other less frequently. When they do it's usually at Benjamin's place because he spends every minute he can spare on the project.

Alexander shows up in his study.

"You hungry?"

"Hm."

It's unclear if that was a yes or a no.

"Well I am, you want me to make something?"

Benjamin looks up.

"You don't have to."

"But you have to eat something and so do I."

"OK."

Alexander's jaw clenches. He disappears into the kitchen. He knows his way around by now, but a few things take him a while to find. He's about to go ask once or twice but keeps deciding against it, trying not to disturb Benjamin.


After they have finished their meal Benjamin goes straight back to his desk. Alexander is standing in the kitchen, eyes closed for a moment. He feels like Benjamin is slipping through his fingers, and it hurts. He'd like to go to him, but he doesn't. It's part pride and part respect for Benjamin's need to focus that holds him back. He cleans up the kitchen and reads a few pages, but he can't quite concentrate. Eventually he packs his stuff and goes to say goodbye. Benjamin smiles and nods. Alexander kisses him and flees to his own apartment.

In the evening he goes for a beer with Paul. He keeps checking his phone, but it stays silent.

"Are you waiting for something?" Paul finally asks, slightly annoyed.

Alexander looks up and shakes his head. He sets his phone to flight mode and puts it away, determined not to be distracted any further.

The next morning he gets up unusually early for a Saturday and goes straight to his practice. By noon he has taken care of every bit of paperwork he could find. His phone is still on flight mode. He's trying to persuade himself that he doesn't want to be disturbed, but deep down he knows he's trying to prove something — to Benjamin and to himself. It's childish, but he can't help it.

Back at his place he turns his phone back on. It's still silent. Benjamin hardly noticed him leaving the day before. That was almost 24 hours ago, and still nothing? Alexander takes a deep breath. This can't go on. He gets in his car and drives to Benjamin's apartment, deliberately *not* calling him first.

At Benjamin's front door he stops and tries to figure out what he's going to say, but his head is completely empty and his throat suspiciously tight.

When he enters the apartment Benjamin is nowhere to be seen. The door to his study is closed. Alexander takes a breath and opens it. Benjamin looks pale and tired. *Might not be a good time.*

"Hey!"

"Hey."

"Did you sleep at all?"

Benjamin rubs his eyes.

"Yeah I did. Not enough though."

"Did you go outside?"

Benjamin exhales. It sounds irritated. He points to a pile of exercise books on his desk.

"These won't mark themselves."

Alexander lowers his gaze. *Might be better to leave him alone.* And then, to his horror, he realises his eyes are welling up. He blinks back the tears. Something in his posture finally gets through to Benjamin. It makes him stand and come over.

"Hey, are you OK?"

And that's it for Alexander's self-control.

"I know what you said, that I had to earn it I mean... but I need you so badly. Can you please take me in your arms?"

His voice betrays how hard it is for him to say that. Benjamin stares at him for a moment before the penny drops. When it finally does he pulls Alexander close and kisses him, wrapping his arms around him and holding him.

"You're an idiot, and so am I, obviously. I'm sorry I couldn't see what you need."

"You've barely looked at me for days, let alone touched me. I crave that, Benjamin. I know we didn't have much sex, but those small caresses — I need that so badly. You'd walk past me and I'd hold my breath, hoping for your hand on my back or maybe even a kiss — and then it's over and it's so painful that I didn't get it. That I'm not worth it."

"Alex. Look at me. The things I say in bed have nothing to do with the way our relationship works! That's just a game! A game that turns both of us on—but it has nothing to do with real life! I love you. I'm sorry I was so caught up in my own world. You don't have to earn anything. Maybe you'll have to kick me once in a while when I'm not getting it. The way you just did."

Benjamin kisses Alexander again, a long, sensual kiss Alexander enjoys no end.

"Come and get what you need if I fail to see it myself. Everything in my power you will get from me, Alexander. I know you want me to do it without being prompted, and ideally I should. But I'm only human."

"No," Alexander says and the beginning of a smile spreads on his face, "you're perfect and must read my mind."

Benjamin gives him a half smile.

"I'm sorry," Alexander whispers. "The drama, I mean. Old baggage, not your fault."

"I'm sorry, too. Wanna tell me?"

Alexander straightens and shakes his head.

"Not worth it. I was just scared. I'm still scared to be honest."

"Scared of what?"

"Of you losing interest. Of being unable to hold your attention. I don't want to lose you, Ben. I love you."

He draws a shuddering breath.

"And on the other hand I'm fully aware of the fact that clingy is unattractive. So I try not to put any pressure on you. To wait for you to come to me."

His voice breaks.

"But I just couldn't stand it any longer."

Benjamin pulls him into his arms.

"Sssshhhh, come here. I just have a crazy work-load. I might be burning the candle at both ends right now, but that's no excuse. Would you please stay tonight? I'll stop working immediately."

"You don't have to. And I'd love to stay. Why don't we order dinner tonight — until it's delivered you can keep working, but then you call it a day?"

"Deal," Benjamin says and kisses him, and a mountain is lifted from Alexander's shoulders.


In the evening they are sitting on the couch, each of them with a glass of wine, talking. Telling each other about their lives — about the things the other one doesn't witness. Alexander finally gets the tenderness he craved so desperately — small casual touches that make him incredibly happy. He puts his head on Benjamin's shoulder and closes his eyes. Neither of them speaks for a while, and then Benjamin draws a breath.

"I've been thinking. About what might convince you that I love you and want to be with you. That I'm not going anywhere."

Alexander straightens and looks at him. Benjamin takes his hands.

"Let's go out. You and me. Dinner, a movie, whatever you want. I don't want you to think I'm ashamed to be seen with you."

Alexander looks at him with affection.

"Thank you. That means a lot. But you don't have to prove anything to me. Are you sure you're there yet? If anyone sees us together and you're outed because of it – are you sure you want that?"

Benjamin hesitates. Alexander kisses him gently.

"It's the thought that counts," he says softly. "I can wait. I'll wait for however long it takes."

"But you would like that, wouldn't you?"

Alexander nods.

"Yeah, I would. But you don't necessarily have to do what I would like you to do."

"No, I don't. I don't have to do what's expected of me, but if I don't there are always consequences. Which I'll have to live with."

Alexander closes his eyes and pulls Benjamin close.

"I am so sorry it's always been like that for you. But would you please believe me when I tell you that I'm different? If I ask you for something, no matter what it is, you can always say no without being punished for it, OK?"

"But you'll be disappointed."

Alexander smiles.

"Yes, probably. But I'm a big boy. I'll live."

"I don't want to disappoint you. I'd like to do this for you. You deserve it. It's really not asking too much, us not hiding any longer. I'm just scared."

"It's OK. I just want to be with you. Doesn't have to be in the wild."

Benjamin relaxes visibly and kisses Alexander's neck.

"I'll make it up to you," he murmurs and his lips wander. Alexander's head falls back.

"You don't owe my anything."

That's the last thing Alexander gets out before Benjamin kisses him full on the lips.

"Can you please shut off that therapist's brain of yours?" Benjamin whispers very close to Alexander's ear, and his warm breath on Alexander's skin causes goosebumps.

"Check."

Alexander grins and simply enjoys Benjamin's warm lips and gentle hands.


"Pool," Benjamin says a while later completely out of the blue.

"Come again?"

"I would like to play pool one day. You and me, a drink or two and a few rounds of pool. Doesn't necessarily look like a date and we could still be together."

Alexander's heart misses a beat.

"That would be amazing, Ben. I would love to!"

"Next weekend, OK?"

Alexander checks his phone and nods. *Is it weird that he has butterflies in his stomach? It's a date. The man he loves is going out with him.* He decides that butterflies are all right, and the anticipation carries him through the whole week.

A week later Alexander is waiting for Benjamin outside the pub, and he's actually nervous. It took him a half hour to decide what to wear and another half hour for his hair. *As if it was the first date. Oh wait. It* is *the first date.* Benjamin shows up and looks gorgeous, and Alexander has to force himself to let go after a brief hug.

"Hey," Benjamin says softly, "you look great!"

Alexander swallows.

"You too."

They go inside and get themselves something to drink, and when the table is free they play a round. Benjamin wins it with ease. Alexander is leaning against the pool table, glass in hand, grinning.

"I'm starting to see why you suggested this."

Benjamin winks at him and shrugs.

"You want revenge?"

"Of course I want revenge."

Alexander positions the balls. When he goes past Ben he whispers:

"At home, at the latest."

Benjamin bites his lip. They play two more rounds which Alexander loses, but that doesn't do any harm to his good mood. They don't touch, not once, always just glance at each other if they make eye contact at all, but the little comments and suggestions going back and forth between them and Benjamin's relaxed laughter are all the foreplay they need. All evening Alexander gets to see the cheeky, playful Benjamin he loves so much.

"I'm falling in love with you all over again," he whispers before going to get them fresh drinks. Benjamin looks after him trying not to seem too obviously enamoured.

# Chapter 20

Christmas draws near, and persuading Benjamin to spend it with the Senne family is surprisingly easy. On Boxing Day Ulrich Senne is called to an emergency so Rahel has a spare concert ticket. She calls Alexander, but he doesn't really feel like it. And then he looks at Benjamin.

"Hang on," he says and covers the handset.

And that's why a little later Rahel Senne and her son's boyfriend are sitting in a concert hall, waiting for the beginning of the Christmas Oratorio.

"I believe my son is quite happy you drew the short straw," she says with a mischievous smile.

Benjamin laughs.

"I don't think it's going to be that short. Thank you for inviting me."

"You're welcome. I'm glad you were free. Do you go to classical concerts a lot?"

"I used to. Haven't in a long time."

*His mother in her black concert clothes, when she performed as part of the choir. A little more colour when she had a solo part. Her flushed cheeks and sparkling eyes at the final applause. She had never seemed happier than on those nights, and she had only shared them with him, never with Chris or his father.*

Benjamin takes a breath. He's not sure if it was a good idea to accept Rahel's invitation. She senses his tension but doesn't ask.

"I haven't seen Alexander like this in a long time. This relaxed. I think he's very happy."

Benjamin doesn't know what to say, but it feels good. Until the concert starts they mainly talk about Rahel's work. Her practice is closed for the holidays.

"I'm really glad not to work at a clinic any more," she says with a sigh. "There are no emergencies at a neurology rehab clinic, but somehow I still ended up working later and different hours than scheduled. Never knowing when you'll get out of work—that's simply too exhausting. My husband handles it surprisingly well, but I never did."

Benjamin nods.

"Are you having a holiday? Not just school holidays I mean but real time off?"

"Pretty much, yeah. The play is finished, we'll start rehearsals after the holidays, but right now it's actually quiet for once."

"That's good," Rahel says with a smile that reminds him of his mother.


When Benjamin comes home Alexander looks at him expectantly.

"Your mum is great," is the first thing Benjamin says.

"I know," Alexander replies, a little surprised.

"Strong, respected, her own boss, and still warm-hearted."

Benjamin puts his arms around Alexander's waist.

"She loves you very much. And it feels like she's extending her love to me. That's nice."

Alexander is touched.

"She likes you. She says I look happy when I'm with you."

Benjamin grins to himself. Alexander rolls his eyes.

"Oh dear. My boyfriend is closing ranks with my mother."

Benjamin's grin widens. Alexander on the other hand turns serious.

"I'm glad you get along so well. My dad might not show it that openly but he likes you, too. They consider you family—because they know I'm serious about you."

"Are you?"

Alexander just nods and kisses him.

"Very," he whispers. "You're the best thing that ever happened to me."


One day Alexander sneaks into the school auditorium while Benjamin is rehearsing with his students. He stays in the background and doesn't believe his eyes when he sees Benjamin on stage. King Henry, played by a young girl with ginger curls, is dressing down Prince Hal—played by Benjamin! Alexander has to fight really hard not to laugh out loud, but the young actress is doing great. Until she tries to stage slap her sassy son. Halfway through the move she bursts out into giggles. Wiping her tears she says:

"I'm sorry, Mr Godan, but I really can't."

Benjamin is laughing just as hard and assures her it's OK.

"You've done it a million times with Florian and it worked every time. You'll be OK. Just make sure you don't accidentally hit him for real — that really hurts, especially when you're not expecting it."

Benjamin looks up and spots Alexander at the back of the auditorium. Benjamin hesitates for a second.

"OK guys, let's take a break. Everybody back in here in 15!"

When the last of the young actors has left, Benjamin saunters towards Alexander.

"Didn't expect an audience," he says with a small smile.

"Hey," Alexander replies but keeps his distance.

"Hey."

Alexander jerks his chin towards the stage.

"Where's your rebellious prince?"

"At the dentist. Had to stand in for him."

Alexander takes a step closer.

"You're glowing."

"I'd forgotten how much I love being on stage."

"You never told me you used to act."

"I really loved it when I was my students' age. My theatre group was like a family, but a functioning one. I really liked that—the corporate feeling, the group effort. I was happy when I was with them."

"Away from home," Alexander adds softly.

"Yeah. Dad hated it of course but Mum put her foot down. As long as my grades didn't slip I was allowed to do theatre."

"Is there footage?"

Benjamin thinks about it for a moment.

"I'm not sure. There are pictures though."

Alexander bats his eyelashes at him and Benjamin rolls his eyes.

"Fine. I'll go find them tonight. Come by?"

"OK."

They hesitate for a second, but then they hug.

"See you later," Alexander whispers and brushes a tiny kiss against Benjamin's temple.


When Alexander makes it to Benjamin's place Benjamin is sitting on the floor of his study surrounded by several boxes, a small one in front of him.

"Oohhh, you found the photos!"

Alexander kisses him quickly and sits down behind him, looking over Benjamin's shoulder. And then something comes to his mind.

"Was it OK for me to come see you at the school today?"

Benjamin leans back against Alexander's chest and closes his eyes.

"For a moment I wasn't coping so well. But then — it was all right. Thank you for being that — circumspect. I was happy to see you."

To Alexander it seems like Benjamin is about to say something else, but he doesn't. Alexander looks at the pile of photos in Benjamin's hand.

"May I?"

Benjamin grins.

"Sure. I've already hidden the worst ones."

Alexander looks through the photos and Benjamin comments. Chris, their parents, classmates. A class photo. And then there are the theatre photos. Benjamin remembers every production and almost every name. A young man with light brown curls stands out. Benjamin lets out a dramatic sigh.

"Oberon… we *all* had a bit of a crush on him."

Alexander chuckles.

"I can't say I'm surprised. Who did you play?"

"Puck of course."

"Of course. Picture?"

Benjamin hesitates.

"Come on."

"Don't you dare laugh."

Alexander kisses Benjamin's neck.

"I won't. I promise. How old were you?"

"Sixteen."

Benjamin pulls out a photo he obviously eliminated from the pile on purpose. Alexander can't take his eyes off it. Benjamin clears his throat.

"I know. After that *everybody* should have been aware I'm bi."

He squares his shoulders.

"It was just for fun though. Just a role."

"Ben," Alexander manages eventually, "this is gorgeous. *You* are gorgeous."

Without being fully aware of it he brushes his fingertips over the photo. Benjamin in profile, his long hair in soft waves, a flower crown on his head and a gentle smile on his lips.

"Can we please not put this away?"

"What, you wanna hang it up?"

"Why not?"

Benjamin doesn't say anything, but he puts the photo on his desk.

Later in bed Benjamin softly says:

"I think I'm there."

Alexander immediately knows what he's talking about. His heart-beat speeds up.

"Are you sure?"

"Yes."

"That's amazing!"

"I mean, I'm scared shitless, but that's not gonna change, is it? So I figured I'll just do it anyway."

He takes a deep breath.

"One of my colleagues invited me to his birthday party and told me I could bring a plus one. Wanna be my plus one?"

Alexander kisses him so passionately Benjamin almost loses track of the conversation.

"Guess that's a yes then."

# Chapter 21

When Benjamin parks his car in front of the birthday boy's place he's more nervous than on the first day at work. A lot more nervous. Alexander takes his hand.

"We don't have to do this. I can still make an exit."

"I don't want you to make an exit. I want you to go in there with me and be your amazing self and sweep them off their feet."

Alexander leans in for a tender kiss.

"I love you. We can do this. I'll let you do the talking so you're in control of the situation, but I'll be there. I'll have your back."

"Don't you dare make a pun about watching my six," Benjamin growls, but Alexander can hear the smile in his voice. Alexander chuckles. Benjamin takes a deep breath and opens the car door.

"Let's do this."


At the front door they run into a middle-aged woman with short blond hair. Benjamin's shoulders tense.

"This is Mylen, she teaches art," he says. "Mylen, this is Alexander, my boyfriend."

Alexander is almost sure he can hear Benjamin's heart beating. He puts his hand on Benjamin's back, supportive and calming. Mylen hesitates for a moment, but then she smiles and shakes Alexander's hand.

"Hi. Nice to meet you."

Benjamin glances at Alexander as they follow Mylen into the building. Alexander smiles and winks at him and Benjamin relaxes visibly.

Charly, the birthday boy is standing at the door to his apartment when all three make it there. He greets Mylen and looks at Alexander.

"Your boyfriend?"

Mylen smiles and shakes her head. Benjamin swallows.

"Erm, no, actually, he's *my* boyfriend. Charly, meet Alexander."

Charly doesn't bat an eyelid and shakes Alexander's hand.

"Come on in everybody!"

Behind Charly there's an athletic looking man with short blond hair. He gives Alexander the once-over and decides to shake his hand but disappears into the apartment as quickly as possible. Alexander rubs little circles on Benjamin's back.

"Breathe," he murmurs.

Benjamin squares his shoulders.

They meet nice and not so nice colleagues, and at one point Benjamin needs a break. They retreat to the balcony and Alexander pulls him into his arms.

"Are you OK?"

"Yeah, I'm fine. It's just—more exhausting than I thought."

"I think you're holding up great, and the majority of your colleagues seem OK."

"Yes, they really are. It will take a while for them to get used to but I'm glad. Relieved."

"That's good."

Alexander kisses Benjamin and he responds to the kiss with more passion than Alexander was prepared for. They startle at an amused clearing of a throat. A slender dark-haired woman in her late twenties is leaning against the balcony door with a broad grin on her face.

"Angelika, right?" Alexander asks.

"Right. How on earth did you memorise all these names that fast?"

Alexander shrugs.

"Anyway, would you gentlemen follow me, please? Charly says dinner is ready."


Most guests are open and friendly with Alexander, only the blond sports coach is reserved and gives him a dirty look a few times.

They barely talk on their way home and when they arrive at Alexander's apartment he pulls Benjamin close.

"Are you OK?"

Benjamin nods.

"Look tired."

"I am," Benjamin says with a sigh. "And I'm a bit scared of Monday."

"Do you regret it?"

"No. And in a way I'm curious to see what happens next. How the rest of my colleagues will react, my students, their parents."

"My guess is that your students will handle it best."


Which is exactly what happens. There are whispers and giggles for a few days and then one of his students — obviously the class agreed on who would have to do it — asks him if the rumours are true. Benjamin confirms it, answers a few questions — mainly about Alexander — and after that it's business as usual for the kids. Benjamin expects negative fallout for a while, but when nothing bad happens he starts to relax and enjoy his new freedom. He and Alexander go out more frequently. Alexander is happy and Benjamin loosens up more and more. They both enjoy the fact that they don't have to hide any more. Dirty looks and hateful remarks are rare. Paul and Benjamin hit it off immediately so they often go out as a group.


Benjamin's Henry play is a huge success, and it's hard to tell who's prouder, the young actors or their director. After the performance Benjamin collapses onto the bed, exhausted but too wired to sleep.

"You remember what you promised me?" Alexander asks.

Benjamin frowns.

"We were planning to get away. Now that the play is done."

"Right!"

"Easter break isn't too far away. Ever been to the French Riviera?"

Benjamin shakes his head.

"My parents have a cottage there…"

Benjamin starts to smile.

"I'd love to. Have you talked to them yet?"

Alexander grins.

"All set. I'm just waiting for you to give me the green light."

"I hereby do," Benjamin whispers and kisses him softly.


Alexander is still smiling when they finally fall asleep.

# Chapter 22

A few days later Benjamin is standing at the window staring outside, silent and absent-minded. He's barely said anything all day. Eventually Alexander can't take it any longer. He puts his book down, gets up and stands behind Benjamin. Putting his arms around Benjamin's waist he says:

"What's up with you?"

"It's just not a good day."

Alexander kisses Benjamin's neck, but Benjamin doesn't react. Alexander thinks back to the day they met. It was a day like this one, one of the first days of spring, sunny, but still cool. And then the penny drops.

"It's the day of her death, isn't it? The date your mother passed away?"

It takes an eternity for Benjamin to nod. Alexander kisses him again.

"Anything I can do?"

"I just want this day to be over."


Benjamin goes to bed early. Not that he's tired, but he just doesn't know what to do with himself. Alexander joins him soon after and pulls him close. He can feel how restless Benjamin is, exhausted, but unable to calm down.

"You didn't visit her grave," Alexander says very softly, anxious not to make it sound like an accusation. Benjamin doesn't answer. And then Alexander realises Benjamin is crying. Silent. Soundless. His tears are soaking Alexander's tee. He pulls him even closer and strokes his hair trying to calm him. It's completely dark outside when Benjamin finally reacts.

"I've never visited her grave."

Alexander can't believe it.

"Why not?"

"Because I'm a failure of a son?"

Alexander sighs.

"What are you scared of?"

Benjamin frees himself from the embrace and rolls onto his back. Alexander kisses his cheek.

"You know you can tell me anything, right?"

Benjamin's eyes are still wet.

"The whole thing is so pathetic I can barely think it. Let alone say it out loud."

"Ben, I love you. There's nothing I want more than for you to trust me. So I can help you."

"What if there is no helping me?"

Alexander gives him a long look.

"Want me to go with you?"

Benjamin doesn't react.

"Do you?"

Benjamin swallows.

"Would you?"

Alexander kisses him again, full on his mouth this time, and Benjamin turns to him and kisses him back.

"Of course," Alexander whispers. "I'd do anything to help you."

"Why?"

"Why? Because that's what partners do. Help each other when one of them isn't strong enough on their own. It's my job, so to say."

Benjamin fights his tears.

"Can we go right now? I know it's a weird time for it but…"

Alexander kisses him again.

"What are you waiting for?" he says with a smile and gets up.

Benjamin smiles back at him.

"How do I deserve you?" he says and sniffs, allowing Alexander to pull him up. Alexander hugs him. They stand like that for a long time, holding each other close.

"I love you so much it hurts," Benjamin murmurs, and Alexander tightens the embrace.

"Let's go." That's all he says when he finally lets go of Benjamin.


When they make it to the cemetery's parking lot Benjamin doesn't move a muscle. Alexander takes his hand.

"My father," Benjamin says out of the blue. "I've always been scared of running into him here. He'd kill me with his bare hands."

"He's not here, Ben."

Benjamin nods and gets out of the car. He straightens. His jaw tenses. Alexander follows him a few steps behind. After a while Benjamin stops, his flash-light pointed at a pale tombstone. He's frozen to the ground. Alexander isn't sure he's still breathing. He carefully puts his hand on Benjamin's shoulder and rubs his back. Benjamin's silhouette seems to shrink. The flash-light is shaking. Without a word Alexander takes it from Benjamin's hand and puts his arm around him.

"It hurts so much," Benjamin whispers. "Seeing her name on this stone. Knowing that everybody who knew her was standing here, saying goodbye. And I wasn't there. What if she was watching and I wasn't there?"

Alexander enfolds him in an embrace.

"She sees you, Benjamin. She sees you now and she saw you back then."

"In prison," Benjamin says, and his voice reeks of disgust.

"Innocent," Alexander responds deliberately calm. "You can't change the fact that you couldn't be here then. But you're here now."

He gently rubs Benjamin's back.

"Do you want some time alone with her?"

Benjamin hesitates, but then he nods and frees himself from the embrace.

"I'll wait in the car," Alexander says and gives him a tender kiss. "Take all the time you need."


The next day Alexander finds a small package at his seat on the dining room table. It's the framed photo of Benjamin as Puck.

'For everything you've done for me, still do for me, are to me. I love you. Ben'

Benjamin's handwriting is blurry all of a sudden.

# Chapter 23

When Benjamin leaves the school and feels the spring sun on his face he spontaneously decides to surprise Alexander—maybe he feels like going out for dinner. Benjamin sneaks into the practice. The door to Alexander's office is ajar, which means there's no patient present. And still Benjamin hears Alexander's voice. He sounds tired.

"Still at the practice, but I'll go home and lay down now. I'm sorry, but I'd be bad company today."

…

"Yeah, again. Third time this month. To be brutally honest—I can't go on."

…

"It's that case I told you about. Today there was—bad news. And then there's my patient at home. I never know what's next with Ben. Sometimes I just don't know what to say any more, and all the experience in the world doesn't help. I love him, but some days I'm not sure I'm strong enough to be with him."

…

"OK. I'll call you."

Benjamin is frozen to the floor. *The patient at home? That's how he sees me?* For a moment he can't move at all, unable to react. And then he turns on his heel and leaves. He won't be a burden to Alexander any longer.

That night Benjamin doesn't hear from Alexander. The next morning Benjamin ignores his phone. When he comes home late at night his answering machine is blinking, but he doesn't check the message. He collapses on his bed and waits for the room to stop spinning.

In the middle of the night he wakes up sweaty and restless. He drags himself out of bed and drinks a glass of water. His hands are shaking, his knees give way. He sinks onto a kitchen chair and studies his hands and arms. The scars remind him how good it feels to have an outlet.

*The feeling when the pressure wears off. Watching the blood run over his skin and wash everything away until his head is empty.*

He clenches his fists. *No.* The still blinking red light on the answering machine catches his eye.

"Hey Benjamin, everything OK with you? I tried reaching you a few times on your mobile. Call me back?"

The message is from 7:34 pm. Benjamin checks the clock. 5:26 am. No use going back to bed. He deletes Alexander's message and goes to take a shower.

When Benjamin gets home Alexander is waiting for him in front of his building. Benjamin's gut clenches. Alexander looks at him quizzically.

"Hey. What's wrong?"

"I have nothing to say to you," Benjamin growls and walks past him.

"Ben, please, what happened?"

Benjamin has unlocked the door and turns back.

"You might wanna think about it some more. Maybe you'll figure it out."

The door slams shut. Alexander stares after Benjamin. He doesn't understand what he might have done wrong. He didn't get in touch for a day, but that's hardly a crime. Besides he had a raging headache that day and he's been trying to explain that to Benjamin. *What am I supposed to do if he doesn't answer his phone and doesn't listen to his messages?* It doesn't make any sense. He unlocks the front door but the key is in the lock at the inside of Benjamin's apartment door. Alexander rings the doorbell. After the third time Benjamin snaps at him from behind the closed door:

"What?!"

"Ben, please. Let me in and talk to me."

No answer.

"Why does everything have to be this dramatic with you?"

After a pause there's an answer, but Benjamin's voice is so distorted Alexander barely recognises it.

"That's just the way it is with us *patients*!"

*What the – oh god.* Alexander closes his eyes. *Please no.*

"Did you come to the practice?" he asks, and his voice breaks. He swallows. "When I was talking to Paul on the phone? Did you hear me?"

"Bingo!" Benjamin's voice reeks of disgust.

Alexander clings to the door for support.

"Please let me in so I can explain it to you," he says as calmly as possible, while there's a storm raging inside him. "Please, Benjamin. I'm so sorry. Please open the door."

It takes forever, but eventually Alexander hears the key turn in the lock. *Thank god.* When Alexander enters Benjamin is leaning against the kitchen door with his back towards Alexander.

"I'm sorry, Benjamin. I shouldn't have said that."

Benjamin turns halfway around.

"I'm more concerned with you *thinking* it!" he growls.

Alexander walks around him. His movements are slow, hesitant. He's unsure if he has any right to be here. Benjamin doesn't react.

"Please, Benjamin. Whatever you need to forgive me, I'll do it. I'm an idiot. I'm so sorry."

"I'm not sure I can forgive this."

"Please don't tell me it's over between us. Please don't. I love you. I can't lose you."

Finally Benjamin looks at him.

"Can you even imagine how much that hurt? Hearing you say that I'm just another patient to you? That you avoid me when you're in bad shape so I can't make it worse? Have you ever considered *telling* me when things are going bad for you? It was the third time of what exactly this month? And why does Paul know about that mysterious case and I don't? Has it ever occurred to you that maybe *I* could help *you* when you need it, not just the other way around? But I guess I'm too weak for that. Unable to withstand stress. Not stable enough."

His voice is trembling with fury. Alexander realises he's fighting to control his temper. Alexander takes one step closer, close enough to touch, but he doesn't.

"I'd had a raging headache all day, for the third time within a month. I could barely think straight and I was feeling sorry for myself, and then I remembered that I was supposed to meet Paul. I called him and cancelled and I whined to him how horrible my life was. That's how it feels to me on days like that — that it's just all too much. That the world should leave me alone. I couldn't go on any longer, and you got hurt in the process. That was unfair. You didn't deserve that, and I shouldn't have said it."

"Maybe you should have called *me* or just generally mentioned the whole thing!"

Alexander hangs his head.

"I didn't want you to see me that way — whiny and irritable."

"I'm not a child, Alexander, and I'm not your patient any more. Give me some credit for fuck's sake."

Alexander looks up.

"That's going to change, I promise."

He swallows.

"If you still want that," he adds in a low voice.

Benjamin sighs and drops onto a chair.

"You're an idiot."

Alexander squats down beside him.

"True. I am."

"But you're *my* idiot."

Alexander looks at him with wide eyes.

"Does that mean — "

"I love you, idiot."

Benjamin bends down and kisses him.

"Don't ever do that to me again," he whispers, and Alexander just nods. He sinks to the floor and puts his head on Benjamin's knee. Benjamin rakes his fingers through Alexander's hair.

"What's up with you?" he asks quietly.

"I just can't take any more."

"What do you mean?"

Alexander is shaking. Benjamin joins him on the floor and pulls him close, trying to calm him down. Alexander kisses him, passionate and demanding. His hands roam Benjamin's body, and then Alexander wraps his arms around him.

"Alexander?"

The concern and the confusion in Benjamin's voice startle Alexander. He pulls himself together.

"I think I might be heading into a burnout."

"Is it—can you talk about it?"

Alexander hesitates. This case has haunted him even after hours, and he didn't even mention it because he didn't want to bother Benjamin.

"If there's anything you need to get off your chest, and if there's a way you can tell me without violating your work ethos, then please for the love of god talk to me."

They sit down on the couch and Alexander is fighting to find the right words. Benjamin just waits, caresses him again and again, gives him time.

"I lost a patient today," Alexander says eventually.

"Wait, what do you mean by 'lost'?"

"She took her own life."

Benjamin is speechless.

"After every session I asked myself if I should commit her. I decided against it every time. It was the wrong call."

Benjamin hugs him and listens. Asks the right questions. Makes the right suggestions. And Alexander breathes more easily. He starts to relax and see more clearly.

"Thank you," he finally murmurs and sighs with relief.

"Didn't do much."

"You did so, so much," Alexander replies and kisses him in gratitude.

# Chapter 24

A few days later Alexander and Benjamin are supposed to have dinner with Paul, but five minutes before they have to leave Benjamin says he won't come.

"But that's OK, you just go on your own."

"I can cancel—or reschedule."

"It's fine. Just go."

Alexander is pretty sure it isn't fine.

"If you want me to stay home—"

"I said"—Benjamin pauses for dramatic effect—"it's fine!"

"Look, I can *see* it isn't, so—"

"Damn it just go on your own!"

And he actually has the nerve to leave the room.

"OK, fine," Alexander calls after him. There's no answer.

"Fine," he repeats to himself. The door shuts behind him with a little more force than necessary. *Great. Very mature, Mr. Therapist.* Alexander hesitates for a moment. But Benjamin would only get more stubborn if he tried again, and he really needs a night out.


The first thing Paul says is:

"No Benjamin?"

Alexander rolls his eyes.

"He's mad at me."

"Did you have a fight?"

"I wish. Benjamin Godan doesn't fight. He just gives you the silent treatment and I hate that. Now I have to guess what's going on. He's expecting me to read his mind."

Paul grins.

"What?!"

"You do realise there's a more mature solution to this?"

"What, you suggest I just ask? Why can't he just say?"

Paul lets out a sigh.

They order their meals and talk about other things, but Alexander is restless and absent-minded. The moment their plates are empty Paul says:

"Go and talk to him already."

"Sorry, Paul. I wasn't very good company tonight."

Paul smiles at him.

"That's OK. Some other time we'll all go out together. Now go take care of your boyfriend."


When Alexander comes home he finds an open vodka bottle on the kitchen table and Benjamin in the bathroom. He's sitting on the floor, a kitchen knife in his hand – and he's bleeding from a dozen thin cuts on his left arm.

"For fuck's sake!"

Benjamin ducks his head. It makes him look like a puppy who's been kicked one too many times. Alexander reaches for a towel and wraps it around Benjamin's forearm.

"Please talk to me. I thought this was long over? That you were over it? Where is this coming from all of a sudden?"

"I don't know," Benjamin says, and it sounds endlessly tired.

"It's not because of — you know, earlier, is it? Is it my fault?"

Benjamin takes a shuddering breath.

"I can't lose you," he says and his voice sounds whiny.

*How much vodka did he have?*

"You won't! What is this about?"

"You were mad at me. I can't — I couldn't handle that. Not when I'm — like this."

"Like what?"

Benjamin looks at him, and he seems to be almost sober all of a sudden.

"Scared, all right? I had a fucking panic attack out of nowhere."

"What? When?!"

Benjamin slumps down.

"Right before we were supposed to leave."

Alexander briefly closes his eyes.

"You didn't want to leave the house because you were having an attack, and you didn't want to tell me because—because of what happened recently."

Benjamin nods.

"You're an idiot," Alexander says and gently kisses Benjamin's temple.

"You would have asked me what caused it and I wouldn't have known and we would have spent the night analysing me," Benjamin mumbles.

"Instead you downed half a bottle of vodka and cut open your arm. I'm not sure that's the better course of action."

He runs a hand through his hair,

"I'm sorry. I know it's not that easy. I just—I would have thought you'd tell me something like that. I thought you know that you can."

"After the whole speech I gave about how I don't want you to see me as a patient and how stable I am yadda yadda—"

Benjamin swallows.

"OK. So what do you want me to do?"

Benjamin looks at him quizzically.

"I get that you don't want me in full therapist mode. So what else do you need me to do? As your boyfriend?"

Benjamin sighs.

"For now, help me take care of the arm please?"

Later in bed Benjamin stares at the ceiling. His voice sounds flat and tired.

"I haven't had an attack in years. It took me by surprise. I didn't know what to do."

He turns to look at Alexander.

"I should have told you."

Alexander caresses his face.

"Please, if it ever happens again—say something."

Benjamin closes his eyes, exhausted beyond measure.

"OK."

# Chapter 25

The night before Easter break they are lying in bed talking—about their upcoming holiday in the South of France, about Alexander's work, about school. Out of the blue Alexander says:

"I found a grey hair this morning."

Benjamin props himself up on his elbow.

"Where?"

"Pulled it out."

That makes Benjamin laugh.

"Seriously?"

Alexander shrugs his shoulders.

"I can see the big forty on the horizon."

"So?"

"I don't know, midlife crisis?"

Benjamin kisses him with abandon. Temple, cheekbone, neck. Alexander closes his eyes and enjoys it. Very close to Alexander's ear Benjamin whispers:

"When you're approaching ninety and I'm just barely in my early eighties we are going to sit on a bench in the sun and bitch about our neighbours."

Alexander swallows. And then he takes Benjamin's face in his hands and gives him a passionate kiss. There's no talk for quite a while. Eventually Benjamin lies back.

"I recently read a few of Shakespeare's sonnets with the eighth-graders."

He looks at Alexander, and his expression is very soft.

"Was thinking of you the whole time," he adds quietly.

Alexander's smile makes his eyes sparkle.

"Shall I compare thee to a summer's day?"

"Yes, amongst others."

"You know that by heart?"

Benjamin closes his eyes.


"Shall I compare thee to a summer's day?
Thou art more lovely and more temperate.
Rough winds do shake the darling buds of May,
And summer's lease hath all too short a date.
Sometime too hot the eye of heaven shines,
And often is his gold complexion dimmed;
And every fair from fair sometime declines,
By chance, or nature's changing course, untrimmed;
But thy eternal summer shall not fade,
Nor lose possession of that fair thou ow'st,
Nor shall death brag thou wand'rest in his shade,
When in eternal lines to Time thou grow'st.
So long as men can breathe, or eyes can see,
So long lives this, and this gives life to thee."

The words linger as if Benjamin's soft baritone had dabbed them in the air with a fine brush. Alexander can't take his eyes off him. He clears his throat to control his voice.

"I think you've never been more beautiful than right now."

Benjamin finally opens his eyes and looks at him. His smile is breathtaking—relaxed and loving. He's at peace with himself and with the world.

"If you can handle more Shakespeare my favourite quote is from Hamlet."

This time he keeps the eye contact and Alexander gets goosebumps.


"Doubt thou the stars are fire,

Doubt that the sun doth move,

Doubt truth to be a liar,

But never doubt I love."


Benjamin's fingertips brush Alexander's cheek.

"I've never felt for anyone the way I feel for you," he says softly. Alexander kisses him again, momentarily speechless, but endlessly happy. His lips wander, and Benjamin allows himself to be spoiled.


Much later they are lying in their ruffled bed exhausted and content.

"Can I ask you something?" Benjamin sounds curious and insecure at the same time.

"Sure."

"I know it's bad form to talk about ex partners, but—"

Alexander raises his eyebrows.

Benjamin goes on:

"Well, you know a bit about some of mine..."

"Let me think—Nele, who was in your class when you came back after the clinic, and originally only wanted to prove you're not gay."

"But then fell for my irresistible charm. Exactly."

Alexander chuckles.

"Angie, close friend whom you wanted to be more than that but who only had eyes for your brother."

"For one night it looked like maybe... but we are digressing."

"Are we?"

"Yes! I wanted to know a little about *your* past!"

When Alexander doesn't answer right away Benjamin regrets the question.

"It's fine if you don't want to," he says quietly.

Alexander takes a breath.

"No, it's all right. My first boyfriend was significantly older than me, and I was still a minor. So we were kinda clandestine. At uni I could finally let off steam, so I did."

"Alexander!"

"What?"

"Who would have thought!"

Alexander shrugs.

"What can I say. We were young."

Benjamin seems to need a moment to digest that information.

"One of my exes you met – unfortunately."

It takes a second, but then the penny drops.

"Oh, yes! Right! He came to the practice, but at that point it was already over, wasn't it?"

"Yes it was but he hadn't quite accepted that yet. Went on like that for a while longer…"

And then Alexander goes very quiet. Benjamin clearly senses the change. He kisses Alexander's forehead.

"It's OK. It's really none of my business actually."

"I want to," Alexander says so quietly Benjamin almost misses it. It's more than obvious that the subject is difficult for Alexander, but he seems determined.

"I've never told anyone about Christian. Paul knew that we were together and so did my parents, but I never talked about our relationship. Not while it lasted and certainly not after it was over."

"Why not?"

"Because it was incredibly complicated."

He runs his hand through his hair.

"He was the first partner who had that dominant streak and—holy shit was that hot. As if I'd finally found the missing piece of the puzzle. All of a sudden everything made sense, and I learned so much about myself."

"Doesn't sound too bad?"

"In theory. Unfortunately what he claimed was dominance was in fact abuse and control. And he hurt me really badly. When I said no to him, which I hardly ever did anyway, I always suffered for it. He let me know that he could always find someone else—and more often than not he did exactly that. So I tried harder to please him, but it was never good enough. It took me far too long to realise how much that relationship was damaging me."

"How long—"

"A little over a year. After that year my self-confidence was so low that it took me another five months to leave him. He'd drilled it into me that I wouldn't be able to find anyone who wanted me. That I had no chance of getting away from him and that I'd come crawling back anyway—but that he'd have found someone better by then."

*"Go ahead and leave. I'll easily find someone else, wouldn't be the first time. Maybe we'll let you watch so you learn something."*

*Flirts and kisses even with Alexander present. The mind blowing sex right after they came home as a reward whenever he had stood back without protest. The mind games. The bottomless bewilderment about what exactly it was that Christian stirred in him. Rage, pain, dependence, helplessness, fascination. Christian's mood swings. His tenderness when he was satisfied with Alexander. His coldness when he wasn't.*

"Alex?"

Benjamin sounds worried. Alexander returns to the present and shakes himself. As if he has to literally shake off the memories and the emotions that come with them. Benjamin looks at him with wide eyes.

"Did I—I mean was anything I said to you ever—"

"A trigger?"

Benjamin nods. Alexander takes a deep breath.

"Some of it, yeah."

Benjamin feels sick.

"I'm sorry, Alexander. I'm so incredibly sorry."

"Not your fault. And it's OK. You have nothing in common with him. You'd never deliberately harm me, I know that, and I trust you. To be honest you defused a few triggers."

"I did?"

"Yes. Sometimes you look at me and say something he used to say, and the fear comes back—but then it's good and you're amazing and you get everything right, and I have reclaimed another piece of myself. With Christian I had to pay a horrible price to get what I wanted. What I needed. With you I get all of that and more… as a gift. Without having to suffer for it. With you my wounds heal, Ben."

Benjamin's throat closes.

"Whenever I say something wrong or you're not doing so well or something's going on in your head that I fail to notice *please* tell me!"

Alexander nods.

"Promise."

"I promise."

Benjamin pulls Alexander close.

"God I'm sorry I brought it up."

"I'm not. I'm glad I could get it off my chest."

Neither of them speaks for a while, and then Alexander takes a breath.

"After that I was single for a very long time. Persuaded myself that I wanted it that way, finding myself and stuff but of course I was mostly just scared."

He starts to smile.

"And then there was Mats. The classic, cliché holiday flirtation. A week on the beach and in bed. We didn't exchange email addresses and I still don't know his last name. But it was such a good time. Carefree. He complimented me and flirted with me all day long and I felt like I was king of the world. In one week he undid so much of the damage Christian had caused… incredible."

"Good man," Benjamin says. He sounds relieved.

"Definitely."

Alexander snuggles up to Benjamin.

"And in a few days time *we* will go for a walk on the beach. I'm in desperate need of a holiday."

"So am I," Benjamin says with a sigh.

Thinking of beaches in Southern France they both fall asleep.

# Chapter 26

Chris is on leave for the first time in a while, so the day before Benjamin and Alexander are due to leave for France the brothers go out for a coffee. As usual Chris can't say much about what he's been doing, but there's something else he wants to talk about.

"I'm starting to get worried about Dad, Benjamin. I hadn't seen him in four months and he's gotten way worse in the meantime."

Benjamin doesn't want to hear it, he never does. But this time Chris insists.

"We have to do something. He can't be on his own for much longer."

So for the first time Benjamin really listens, and he can't help but get worried, too. Their father fell, again, no fractures this time. But he seems to be disoriented from time to time, and it's getting worse, according to Chris.

"I think we should get him help."

Benjamin huffs out a breath.

"As if he'd agree to that."

"I'm not so sure. He doesn't admit it but I think he knows he needs help."

"OK, fine then. Get him a nurse."

"I will. But I need you to check in when I'm not here. Please?"

Benjamin's jaw sets.

"Do it for me?"

Chris sighs.

"At least call the nurse once a week. Let me give her your number in case of an emergency."

Benjamin gives him a resigned nod.

"Yeah OK."

"Thanks, Brother."

And then Benjamin straightens.

"I've something to tell you, too."

"OK?"

"I'm seeing someone."

"Cool! I wanna know everything about her!"

Benjamin bites his lip.

"Him."

That makes Chris pause for a moment, but then he gives his little brother a wide grin.

"Fine then, him."

"Really? Just like that? No fuss?"

"You're my brother, and I love you. I want you to be happy. God knows you deserve it."

So Benjamin tells his brother about the guy Chris vaguely remembers as one of the people who helped Benjamin move, and he even explains how they originally knew each other. Chris stays silent for a moment and then says:

"Ask him to join us. I wanna meet him."

"Well, technically you did meet him..."

Chris just gives him a patented older brother look. It makes Benjamin chuckle.

"OK fine, I'll call him."

Chris takes a sip of coffee.

"Gotta give him the talk."

Benjamin stares at him.

"What, 'make sure to get him home by 9'?"

"No. More like 'if you hurt my little brother, I'll break your nose, welcome to the family'."

The three men have dinner together and Alexander and Chris, as different as they are, get along well. After they have finished their meal Chris tries to persuade Alexander to come to a club with them, but Alexander politely declines.

"One of us has to be fit to drive to the South of France tomorrow, and besides you see each other not nearly often enough. Just go have fun."

He kisses Benjamin goodbye very chastely and offers his hand to Chris. Benjamin's older brother shakes it firmly.

"It was nice meeting you, Alexander. Hope I'll see you around."

"Likewise." Alexander smiles at him and watches them leave. He's still smiling when he makes it back to his place, happy the encounter went that well. He knows how much Benjamin loves his big brother, even though growing up with him wasn't always easy. But it's good to see how close they are now.

A few hours later Alexander's phone rings, and it takes him forever to realise that it *is* his phone. Eventually he drags himself out of bed and picks it up.

"Alexander? It's Chris."

Alexander's sleepy annoyance turns into fear at the sound of Chris' voice.

"What happened?"

"I need you to come to the hospital as quickly as possible. Benjamin's injured, he's unconscious, and they can't tell if he'll make it."

Alexander can't breathe.

"Alexander? Are you coming?"

"On my way," he forces himself to say and almost drops the phone. His hands have never shaken so badly before. *I can't drive like this. It's the middle of the night. Paul is on holiday.*

He calls his parents. Ten minutes later his dad is there to pick him up. Of course he wants the medical details, but Alexander doesn't know anything. All he knows is that the man he loves might be dying. Might already be dead by the time he makes it there. His hands just won't stop shaking.

When they arrive at the hospital, Alexander's dad makes a bee line for Intensive Care. The nurse on duty looks surprised.

"Dr. Senne? What—"

"Benjamin Godan?"

"Erm, he's just gotten out of surgery, number 2."

Before she can protest Dr Senne says quietly but firmly:

"He's family," and gestures to Alexander to follow him.

When they enter the room, Chris stands and greets them quietly. Alexander doesn't hear what Chris is telling his father. He can only stare at Benjamin's bruised face. He's so pale, so still. His slender hands are bruised, too. *A fight? He was in a fight? Did something happen at the club?* Alexander sinks down on the chair Chris vacated earlier. He barely notices his dad leave, presumably to talk to his colleague. He does notice Chris' hand on his shoulder.

"What happened?" Alexander whispers.

"We were at the club. He wanted to get some fresh air, I wanted to stay inside. He got into a fight, and he's been stabbed."

Alexander feels like he's about to have a breakdown. Chris squats down by his side.

"Alexander? Did you hear me?"

Alexander clears his throat.

"Yes. What do the doctors say?"

"They can't tell us much. It's a gut wound, his heart and lungs are OK but he lost a lot of blood and – it's possible we got here too late. They say he could wake up any moment, or – not."

Chris stands and turns away from Alexander. His voice is strangled when he goes on:

"He was unconscious when I found him. He was so still, and covered in blood, and because it's Benjamin I couldn't remember any of my training and didn't even check properly and I thought – I thought I'd lost my little brother. It could still happen any moment."

Alexander looks at Chris for the first time. Benjamin's brother is so tense he might snap any minute. His skin looks ashen under his tan, and his hands are curled into fists, knuckles white. Chris is a man of action, and here he's absolutely useless. There's nothing he can do. Strength, skills, resilience, none of his abilities are of any use here.

"Thank you for calling me," Alexander says softly.

Chris just nods.

"Can I – would you please give me a moment alone with him?"

For a second it looks like Chris is about to yell at him, but then he just nods again and leaves. And Alexander can't keep the tears at bay any longer. He reaches for Benjamin's hand and gently brushes his thumb over Benjamin's knuckles.

*Bruised knuckles. Because Benjamin had put his fist through a wall again and again.*

He looks up at Benjamin's face, and it's physically painful to see him like that. The force necessary to do that much damage to a face makes Alexander swallow. He tastes bile. *Brain damage! Chris didn't say anything about brain damage, or did he?!*

"Ben, please," he whispers, running his fingertips over Benjamin's temple. "I'm here. Please wake up and look at me. Please?"

There's no reaction. Alexander starts laughing hysterically when he realises he can't remember the colour of Benjamin's eyes. Well, they're blue of course, but what exactly do they look like? He can't remember, and it drives him crazy. Emotional breakdown. That's what this is. He's losing his grip.

# Chapter 27

Neither Chris nor Alexander can be persuaded to leave the hospital, so Dr Senne makes them promise to take turns sleeping. Alexander silently hugs him.

"Let me know if you need anything."

Alexander nods.

"Thank you," Chris murmurs.


Morning comes with no change. The doctors look worried but don't say much. Chris is so restless Alexander almost *orders* him outside. There's no change. In the afternoon Alexander leaves for a quick shower and change of clothes, worried sick that something might happen while he's gone. But there has been no change by the time he comes back. He and Chris have fallen into a routine of dozing, short walks, coffee, and sitting with Benjamin. Alexander keeps talking to him in a low, gentle voice. At one point he's reading Shakespeare to him, from the sonnets. Chris just stares at Benjamin's face, trying to will him into consciousness. Nothing works. Time stands still. They don't talk much, just trade tired, pained looks. There's nothing to say. They make it through another night.


It's dawn and Alexander is asleep when finally there's a change.

"Alexander," Chris calls out under his breath.

Alexander sits up and rushes to Benjamin's bedside. It takes forever, but eventually Benjamin opens his eyes. As much as possible that is.

"Alexander," he murmurs. "The bastard got to me."

"What? Who?" Chris demands.

Benjamin closes his eyes again.

"Long story."

Alexander's stomach drops.

"What? Are you saying—Brunner?"

Benjamin gives the slightest nod.

"Who's Brunner?!"

"Like he said, long story."

"Alexander, if you know who did this to him, I swear to God if you don't tell me right away—"

"Please," Benjamin whispers, "don't do anything rash. Get me the police. I want to make a statement. They'll get the fucking son of a bitch and put him away for a very long time. Let him rot in prison. Hope someone fucks him really hard."

Chris looks at Alexander over Benjamin's still form with thunder in his eyes.

"Fuck the police. *I* will put him away. For eternity."

Alexander shakes his head.

"Ben is right. Not worth it."

He looks at Benjamin.

"I reckon the authorities will want to talk to you anyway as soon as the doctors say you're able to."

Silence falls over the room as Alexander and Benjamin look at each other with tiny smiles. Chris clears his throat.

"I'll get the doc."

When they are alone Alexander takes Benjamin's hand.

"You scared me to death."

"Sorry."

"I love you so much I can't even — if I'd lost you — "

Benjamin gives Alexander's hand a little squeeze.

"You didn't. I'm a tough cookie."

Alexander chuckles and it turns into a sob.

"God I need to kiss you."

"Careful."

Alexander leans in and places gentle kisses on the corner of Benjamin's mouth, his cheekbone and his temple. Benjamin's eyes close.

"This feels good."


Brunner is arrested the same day. A witness at the club saw him follow Benjamin outside, and given their backstory this time the authorities believe Benjamin's statement: Brunner brutally attacked him at the club's back door, claiming Benjamin had it coming. 'An eye for an eye, only *you* aren't going to walk away from this,' Benjamin remembers him saying before he lost consciousness.

It takes a lot of time, but Benjamin makes a full recovery. On his first day back in school his students have decorated the classroom. He doesn't want to talk about what happened but the kids know anyway. They keep asking if he's OK, and they are on their best behaviour.

Things return to normal, except for Benjamin's nightmares. By now Alexander knows what they are about. He dreams of being choked or stabbed, unable to move, unable to defend himself, and there's always that horrible, paralysing threat of being abused. The night before Benjamin has to appear in court is the worst. He wakes up drenched in sweat, every muscle in his body tense, and he's shaking. Alexander suggests taking a bath, but Benjamin barely reacts.

"Ben? Please?"

Alexander manages to get him to the bathroom and into the tub. He hesitates for a moment but then gets in, too. He starts massaging Benjamin's neck and shoulders, and finally some of the tension leaves Benjamin's body. Leaning back against Alexander's chest he lets out a breath.

"This is pathetic, Alex."

"I can't even begin to imagine what you must feel like. But it's almost over."

"I'm scared of him," Benjamin says, and it sounds almost surprised. Like he's just come to that conclusion. "I know he's in jail and once he's sentenced he won't get out for a long time, if ever. And still I shit my pants at the thought of having to be in the same room. Pathetic."

"He almost killed you, Ben. Threatened you. Twice. The first time he got away with it. Of course you're scared. You're worried, on some level, that he might get away with it again. Hurt you again."

Benjamin goes very still. He swallows hard.

"He can't, right? They'll put him away?"

Alexander's throat is completely dry all of a sudden. He wraps his arms around Benjamin.

"Yes, they will. He can't hurt you ever again."

Benjamin doesn't say anything for a long time. Then he takes a breath.

"I wish Chris could be there."

"I know. I'm sorry he can't."

Chris is on one of his missions, presumably abroad. Benjamin hasn't talked to him for weeks.

"Where's that big brother when you need him?" Benjamin says, but there's a smile in his voice.

"Taking care of things elsewhere," Alexander replies. It's an old joke. Chris doesn't like the official language regulations. He says they remind him of Bond movies. He rather calls it 'taking care of things.'

"Good thing *you* are here, taking care of *me*."

"Always," Alexander murmurs.

# Chapter 28

When the trial is over and Brunner is sentenced, Benjamin finally gets some peace. He sleeps better and breathes more freely, and eventually Alexander stops treating him with kid gloves.

"I feel like we deserve a holiday," Alexander says one evening.

Benjamin looks up from his book.

"True. We were about to go to France..."

"I could ask my parents if we can have the cottage during summer break."

Benjamin smiles at him.

"Sounds good. Oh but don't they want to go there themselves in the summer?"

"There's only one way to find out."

Alexander gets up to take his phone, but Benjamin holds him back.

"Wait a second. We could — all go together."

Alexander looks at him surprised.

"Are you sure you want that?"

"Don't you?"

Alexander bends down and gives him a gentle kiss.

"That would be wonderful. I'm just not sure if you can handle that much family."

Benjamin gives him an open, happy smile, one of those that make his eyes sparkle.

"Your family is amazing. I have a lot of family to catch up on… I'd *love* to go on a holiday with them."

Alexander smiles back and kisses him again.

"OK. One family holiday in the French Riviera. Coming up."


Alexander's parents are a little surprised at Benjamin's suggestion, too, but they like it, so shortly after, the four of them fly to the South of France. When they arrive Alexander closes his eyes and takes a deep breath. His mother smiles at him.

"You haven't been here in forever."

"But I remember it well. Smells like the French Riviera."

Benjamin takes his hand and they look at each other.

"Welcome to my home away from home." Alexander grins and turns to his mother.

"*Why* haven't I been here in forever, Mum?"

Rahel Senne shrugs her shoulders.

"Not cool, I assume."

"*I* assume it's been ages since you went on holiday," Benjamin says.

Alexander's father hums affirmatively.

Alexander puts his arm around Benjamin's shoulders.

"True. So it's high time for a little savoir vivre."


An old friend of the family picks them up at the airport and drives them to their cottage. While Alexander's parents open windows and put away suitcases, Alexander shows Benjamin around the house. Benjamin pauses at the pool. The cottage is located on a hillside, so the terrace gives a view of the village and the sea.

"This is incredible, Alex. So, so beautiful."

Alexander hugs him from behind and rests his chin on Benjamin's shoulder.

"Little surprise courtesy of my parents: they will leave before we do. For the last few days all this will be ours alone."

Benjamin turns in Alexander's arms.

"What? They don't have to do that!"

"But they want to. And I think it's a good idea. Just you and me, the sun, the beach and the pool. Let me enjoy that. With you."

Benjamin gives him a long kiss. Which is brought to an end by an amused cough.

"You boys want us to leave right away?" Ulrich Senne is grinning.

Benjamin blushes.

"Of course not!"

And then Alexander's mother joins them on the terrace.

"I don't know about you guys but I'm hungry. Going out for dinner in an hour?"

They spend glorious days at the beach and on the terrace, go out for dinner or cook together, invite their neighbours and are invited themselves. When Rahel and Ulrich finally pack their bags, they say their goodbyes with mixed feelings.

"Thank you for everything," Benjamin says when he hugs Rahel.

"You're welcome. Enjoy the rest of your holiday, you deserve it. See you at home!"

And then they are finally alone. They are sitting on the terrace, drinking wine and watching the sunset over the sea, and at some point Benjamin gets up and jumps in the pool.

"I've always wanted to swim in a pool at night. They never let you in a hotel!"

Alexander grins and watches him, half empty wine glass in hand. Benjamin is doing his lengths, calm and powerful, and Alexander can't remember ever being happier in his whole life. Eventually Benjamin pauses and puts his arms on the edge of the pool. Looking up at Alexander he says:

"Come in!"

"Way too cold."

"Sissy," Benjamin snorts and splashes water at him.

"Hey!"

Alexander puts down his glass and jumps in the pool. The playful hand to hand fight that ensues predictably ends in a passionate kiss.

"It's really cold," Alexander complains after two minutes.

"You need to take some exercise."

"I'd rather exercise somewhere else."

Benjamin chuckles and kisses him.

"OK, OK. You win. How about a hot shower and a comfy bed?"

Alexander closes his eyes.

"Hmmm. Sounds good. Very good."


A little later they are lying in bed looking at each other.

"This is what I've been waiting for all the time," Alexander murmurs. "Just you and me."

They kiss with tenderness and devotion. The house is theirs, they don't have to consider anyone else, they can let go, and they have all the time in the world. Alexander's lips wander over Benjamin's warm skin, and they both enjoy it to the fullest.


The next evening they go out for dinner and then to a bar for a few drinks. Benjamin is relaxed and openly shows his affection, and Alexander couldn't be happier. Until someone bumps into him. Three men in their late twenties plant themselves in front of Alexander and Benjamin threateningly. Benjamin's French isn't good enough to understand the exact words but the meaning is clear. They seem to be of the opinion that Benjamin and Alexander have no business at "their" bar. Alexander tries to defuse the situation, but that only infuriates the three even more, and suddenly the leader lashes out. Alexander falls—and Benjamin sees red. It only takes the staff a few minutes to call security, but during that time Benjamin gives as good as he gets. Security interferes and the three men are thrown out of the bar. Alexander's lip is bleeding. Benjamin looks significantly worse but refuses to go to the hospital. Both of them just want to go home. A staff member calls them a taxi—compensation, he's very sorry—and they silently ride back. Alexander disappears to the bathroom immediately. Benjamin falls onto the bed and closes his eyes.

When Alexander emerges from the bathroom and slips between the sheets without a word, Benjamin looks at him.

"You're considering this falling back into old patterns, right? I should probably have kept my cool and waited for security, but—"

He runs his hand through his hair.

"I know you prefer solving stuff like that verbally. I'm sorry, OK?"

Alexander doesn't react. Benjamin feels awful.

"Please say something."

Alexander swallows.

"That's not the point. You didn't do anything wrong."

"Then why aren't you talking to me?"

Finally Alexander looks at him, and there are tears in his eyes.

"Because I don't know what to say. My mind is racing. I feel like I was completely caught off guard. Overwhelmed, useless, and—"

Benjamin raises his eyebrows—and flinches. Alexander looks at him, alarmed.

"Oh god I didn't even ask how you're feeling! Are you sure you don't need a doctor?"

Benjamin shakes his head.

"A shower, two paracetamol and a bit of sleep."

Alexander looks at him hesitantly for a moment.

"OK, if you say so?"

"It's not my first rodeo."

It sounds more flippant then Benjamin intended. He takes a deep breath.

"Sorry. Be right back."


In the shower Benjamin closes his eyes and lets the warm water wash over his face. As the blood is washed away so is part of his anger and insecurity, and the pain lessens a bit. He craves Alexander's touch. The weird atmosphere between them is choking him. Just as he turns off the water there's a knock, and Alexander pokes his head in.

"Can I come in?" he asks softly.

"Of course!"

Benjamin wraps a towel around his waist, and Alexander approaches him. His eyes are on the floor. It takes a moment before he looks at Benjamin. But then he reaches out and carefully touches Benjamin's cheek, his forehead, temple, lower lip—all the little cuts and bruises. Benjamin tries his best not to flinch. Alexander's gaze is glued to Benjamin's mouth.

"Can I—I'd like to kiss you."

Benjamin suppresses a sob and nods. Alexander closes his eyes and carefully kisses him. Obviously he forgot that his own lip is split, too, because he lets out a startled little sound that makes Benjamin chuckle. He rests his forehead against Alexander's and pulls him into his arms.

"What's up with you?" Benjamin whispers.

And that's it for Alexander's self-control. He squeezes Benjamin tight and buries his face in the crook of his neck. Benjamin strokes his back and softly talks to him. Eventually Alexander calms down enough for them to part. Benjamin frames Alexander's face with both hands, kisses him gently and says:

"Let's get some sleep. I'm dead on my feet."

Alexander hesitates briefly, but then he nods.


In bed Alexander turns to Benjamin.

"I know you're tired, but I'd still like to try and explain it."

Benjamin nods. Alexander turns onto his back and looks at the ceiling.

"It's—complicated. I was mad because they ruined our evening. Scared that it might have ruined the whole holiday. I'm sorry it happened *here*. You wouldn't be here if it wasn't for me wanting to come here. And I was so helpless. It's been so long since something like this happened to me, and I was paralysed. And I didn't want you to get in a fight for me."

Benjamin grimaces.

"I know. You're right."

"No, I mean—shouldn't I be capable of defending myself?"

He looks at Benjamin. Benjamin's smile turns to something bordering on smug.

"I'd happily fight for you again any day."

Alexander's expression is unreadable. He keeps looking at the ceiling.

"I think that's the major problem with the whole thing."

"Huh?"

"I—can't admit to myself that—"

He sighs and looks directly at Benjamin.

"I liked it."

Benjamin is speechless.

"Seeing that you're capable of defending me. Stupid as it sounds but that feels good. It's—hot."

His voice is so low Benjamin barely understands him.

"Seeing you fight was hot."

A wide grin spreads on Benjamin's face, and he doesn't even care about his lip being split anew.

"Nice to see you're amused," Alexander says with a pout.

Benjamin chuckles softly and pulls him close.

"Admitting that must have been so hard. I assume there's a perfectly good psychological explanation for it. I reckon the keyword is dominance. But whatever, fact is I'd do anything for you, and I couldn't care less if it earns me a bloody nose."

"Isn't that pathetic? Me being in need of saving I mean."

"Alex, that's not your world. You're too good for that."

"And you're not?"

Benjamin shrugs. Alexander kisses him with devotion.

"Thank you. For doing it when it's necessary. I hope it won't ever be necessary again but it's — it feels good to know that you can. Safe. Secure."

Benjamin smiles at him and kisses him back.

"Hell on the ego," Alexander adds with a dramatic sigh that makes both of them laugh.

"Good night," he says shortly after and kisses Benjamin one last time.

"Good night," Benjamin replies with a happy smile on his face, half asleep already.

# Chapter 29

A few weeks later the day finally comes when Benjamin's father can't stay in his house any longer. Benjamin talks to his father's physician. The doctor says his father needs nursing and supervision twenty-four-seven.

"I assume neither you nor your brother are able or willing to provide that, are you?"

Benjamin shakes his head. The idea of spending all day with his father makes him sick. And still he feels guilty. No matter how many times he's said or thought 'He's not my father' in his life — it's not that easy.

"My brother is on active service, I'll have to make that decision on my own. My father will fight me tooth and nail."

"Do you want me to talk to him?"

Benjamin sighs in relief.

"Please. Maybe he will listen to you. He certainly won't listen to me."

Benjamin finds room for his father in a care home, and eventually his father reluctantly agrees to move there. Right after taking him there Benjamin drives to Alexander's place, goes to the living room and collapses on the couch. Alexander squats down.

"That bad?"

"You should have heard him. He kept saying 'If Christoph was here, he wouldn't allow this!' and that I had no right to do it to him. That I was doing it behind his son's back to take his house. That Chris would come to free him and then I'd get what I deserve."

"He's demented, Ben. He doesn't know what he's saying."

"It's not too far from what he used to say when he was perfectly sane."

The bitterness in Benjamin's voice breaks Alexander's heart.

"What can I do?"

Benjamin just shakes his head, exhausted.

"Nothing. It's better like that. There is no other way."


And then Chris is finally home for once. Something exploded too close to his face. He needed surgery on his eye, but the doctors say his eyesight will be fully restored. He's on medication, which is why he turned down the beer Benjamin offered to buy him in favour of coke. Benjamin thinks that's very funny, probably because he himself is on his third beer. They talk about their father but soon enough Benjamin wants to change the subject, and they end up discussing Angie. She has a new job and will be moving back.

"You used to have quite the crush on her, but I guess that's in the past now, with you driving stick these days?"

"Yup. I still think she's great though. *She* used to have a crush on *you*, you know that, right?"

Chris chokes on his coke.

"She what?"

"Oh please. She wouldn't even notice me because she was busy making moon eyes at *you*!"

Chris goes very silent at that.

"You really didn't know, did you?" Benjamin asks softly.

"No. I thought—I wasn't really sure she was into guys at all. She used to be such a tomboy!"

"But you like her."

Chris blushes a little.

"Well, I hear helping people move is the way to get a date nowadays." Benjamin grins.

Chris doesn't really say much for the rest of the evening, but a few days later Benjamin gets a cryptic text from Angie that sounds like Chris has made a move. Benjamin grins to himself while reading the message a second time. Very good. Those two would make a great couple.


Chris' and Angie's may-or-may-not-be a relationship has been going on for three weeks, much to Benjamin's amusement—because he gets texts and calls from both parties on a regular basis—when there's a call that makes him go numb. It's his father's care home, and they are asking him to come as soon as possible. Chris is already on his way they say. It's serious. Benjamin doesn't move a muscle, phone still in hand. Without really thinking he types a message to Alexander:

'My father is dying.'

Belatedly he realises Alexander is probably in a session and won't check his phone. He considers calling his office but doesn't. He's stalling. And he doesn't want to go on his own. Taking a breath he tells himself Chris will be there and finally gets going.


Chris is sitting by their father's bedside when Benjamin gets there. Chris looks up and stands so they can hug.

"What's the news?" Benjamin asks without looking at his father's face.

"He's unresponsive, but they say he has lucid moments from time to time, so who knows..."

Benjamin pulls another chair close and sits down on the other side of the bed, and together they wait for one of those moments. There's exactly one.


Something in the atmosphere of the room has changed. Benjamin looks up and realises his father is looking directly at him.

"Benjamin."

Chris straightens when he hears the quiet, broken voice of his father. His father turns to him.

"Christoph."

The brothers look at each other. Chris gets up and walks around the bed. With his hands on Benjamin's shoulders he stops.

"Father."

"You're here. You're both here. My sons."

Benjamin's eyes get wet. Chris' hands briefly squeeze his shoulders.

"How do you feel?" Chris asks.

"Tired. I'm so incredibly tired."

He looks at Benjamin.

"Would you give us a moment please?"

Benjamin's throat closes. These might very well be the last moments of their father's life and he's not allowed to be there. He starts to get up but Chris won't let him.

"Christoph." That's all their father says, and he's his old military self all of a sudden.

Benjamin shrugs off Chris' hands and flees.


He doesn't go far. He knows he should leave, leave the care home behind, the father who even now won't accept him, but he can't. He thinks it's pathetic, but deep down he still hopes for his adopted father's love. He sits down on a chair in the hallway and leans his head against the wall. He refuses to cry but it takes all his strength. And then all of a sudden Chris is sitting next to him.

"He wants to talk to you alone," he says quietly.

Benjamin stares at him.

"What?"

"He wanted a moment with me and now he wants the same thing with you. I'm sorry he didn't say that right away, Ben."

Tears are running down Benjamin's cheeks now.

"I can't."

"Yes. You can. I'm right here around the corner."

Benjamin takes a few deep breaths and wipes away the tears. Chris nods at him.

"I'm here."


When Benjamin re-enters his father's room he's already waiting. Benjamin sits down, unable to look his father in the eyes.

"Benjamin," his father says quietly. "I'm so glad you're here. I thought you wouldn't come."

Benjamin doesn't know what to say to that.

"I wasn't a good father to you, I know that. It was so easy with Christoph, he's like me. With you — I never knew how to talk to you. And you remind me of you mother so much I can barely take it."

"Father." Benjamin swallows and moves his chair closer to the bed.

"I'm sorry, Benjamin. I know how often I went wrong, and I'm sorry."

They look at each other, and Benjamin starts to smile. They don't talk much after that, but the things they do say are overdue. Eventual Benjamin's father sinks back into his pillow and closes his eyes.

"Would you please go get your brother?"

The brothers are sitting at their father's bedside, and the last thing their father says is:

"I love you, my sons."

When everything is over the brothers sit down on a bench in the park behind the care home. Benjamin's emotions are running wild and his head is empty. They talk about the funeral. And then there's a long pause. Benjamin swallows.

"I'm sorry I wasn't at Mother's funeral."

"You were locked up at the time."

Benjamin looks at his boots.

"They would have let me attend. Two guards and cuffs, but I could have been there."

Chris' head snaps up.

"Then why weren't you?!"

"Father didn't want me there. *You* probably didn't want me there. You'd lost your mother because of me."

*"We'd* lost *our* mother, Benjamin!"

Benjamin's voice sounds strangled.

"I had no right to be there. Her death was my fault."

"No, it wasn't. We'll never know what happened before she left, why she had that accident. Just stop with the guilt trip for heaven's sake!"

Chris turns his body towards Benjamin so he can fully look at him.

"I did want you there, Ben. Father was a mess, I'd never seen him like that before. And I had just lost my best friend on a mission he shouldn't even have been part of."

He takes a shuddering breath.

"I would have needed my brother to lean on."

Benjamin stares at him, unable to process what he just heard. And then he starts to cry.

"I'm sorry," he says. "I'm sorry, Chris. For not being there. For not making the effort. For making you worry over me, and over Father, when you probably needed your head in the game over there. I'm sorry for not being a brother."

Chris shakes his head, his eyes bright with tears as well, and pulls Benjamin into a hug.

"You've always been my brother, and you always will. You're all I have left, Ben."


When Benjamin comes home, Alexander just gets up and wraps his arms around him.

"I'm so sorry, Ben."

They stay like that for a long time, and then Alexander leads Benjamin to the living room, his arm still around Benjamin's waist. Benjamin is an orphan now, for the second time in his life. And Alexander isn't sure what to say. They sit down and Benjamin snuggles up to him, desperate for his touch. After a while he lays down with his head in Alexander's lap, eyes closed.

"He's gone. All the anger and hurt, and now that he's gone… before he died… I told Dad that I'd realised they gave me a good life. I'm glad I got the chance to do that. Before it was too late."

Alexander simply waits. Benjamin opens his eyes with a sigh.

"I know you're dying to ask me all those clever questions that will eventually help me untangle my daddy issues, but… please don't make me talk right now, OK? Just let me be silent in your arms?"

Deeply moved Alexander leans in to kiss his forehead.

"Anything you want, Ben. Whatever you need."

# Bonus Material

Think of this book as a movie. It is in my head anyway. If this was a DVD (or Blu-ray, I'm moving with the times), *here* would be the bonus section. For a couple of reasons that material *isn't* in the book, but don't fret, it's easily accessible if you own a device that is hooked up to the net.

Just go to:

https://a-brighter-world.de.tl

and stay in the Brighter World for a little longer. Admittedly some of it is quite dark…

Content warning:

My boys are kinky bastards, so if you're not into BDSM you should probably just leave the story as it is in the book. It works perfectly fine that way!

Thank y'all for coming on this roller coaster journey with me and the boys!

Zeitfracht Medien GmbH
Ferdinand-Jühlke-Straße 7
99095 Erfurt, Deutschland
produktsicherheit@kolibri360.de